The Incredible Benefits of Knowing God

by

David Blunt

Publishing assisted by:

Insight International
P. O. Box 54996
Tulsa, OK 74155

Unless otherwise noted, all Scripture quotations are from
the King James Version of the Bible.

Scripture quotations marked NIV are from the Holy Bible,
New International Version. Copyright © 1973, 1978, 1984,
International Bible Society. Used by permission.

Scripture quotations marked AMP are from the Amplified
Bible. Copyright © The Lockman Foundation, 1958. Used
by permission.

Contents

Dedication

To my wife, Kim, and my two sons,
Daniel and Stephen.
To God be the glory.

INTRODUCTION

DON'T FASTEN YOUR SEAT BELT

"He is a miserable man who knows all things, and does not know God; and he is happy who knows God, even though he knows nothing else. But he who knows God and all else beside is not made more blessed thereby; for he is blessed through God alone."
ST. AUGUSTINE

Thousands of people travel by plane from one destination to another. For a few hours, people crowd into three–across seats among total strangers. Sandwiched between a window and an aisle seat, the middle person has the challenging task of trying to drink a soda and eat peanuts without spilling or dropping anything while keeping his arms off the armrests taken over by his neighbors.

These random meetings seldom produce more than pleasant greetings without any further conversation. Even when conversations are initiated, they often focus on jobs, weather, stock markets, news, or the perils of constant travel. Conversations seldom dive beneath the surface of polite exchanges of information and into the deep waters of really knowing one another.

Total strangers on planes may talk for a while, share a meal together, and even watch a movie, but nothing about their lives is changed by these brief encounters.

However, on rare occasions, two people on an airplane connect. They move beyond the formal greetings and polite conversations to real dialogue about life. At times, some people find it easier to share intimate details about themselves with total strangers when they would never share such things with people they know. Knowing they will never meet again, these strangers counsel and advise one another in the safe cocoon of a plane forty–thousand feet in the air. No one else can hear their conversation. And after a few hours, they will depart in total anonymity with their shared secrets safely locked in a stranger's mind never to be shared again.

Let me ask you: Do any of these people really come to know one another? With few exceptions, will they ever form a relationship or develop any lasting connection? Can we ever say that a few moments of talking to someone on a plane reaches the level of truly knowing that person? I think not.

But wait. Something very similar happens weekly in another form of travel. Spiritual flights of one to two hours happen every Sunday in churches all over our country. People from all walks of life stream into a church, politely greet one another, and rarely engage in meaningful conversation.

Yes, they share a common experience with one another. Songs are sung, and instructions are given. Announcements are made, and even shaking hands or hugging one's immediate neighbors is encouraged. But rarely does a conversation lead to intimate details or revealing confessions for fear that after the service the private confessions might be shared publicly at a nearby restaurant or broadcast inappropriately through gossip and innuendo.

However, spiritual flights are not about meeting other people and talking about their lives, though such fellowship is important and necessary. Something significant is supposed to happen on these flights—it's called worship. In such encounters, one should rise above mundane daily routines and enter into communion with the Someone other than the persons sitting around him. Such times are for meeting God.

And I hope that more than simply meeting God occurs. Perhaps a conversation called prayer will take place with Him. Prayer in which the human one tells the divine One all about the intimate details of life. Yet, is such a conversation necessary if the divine One really does know everything there is to know about the human one?

Or perhaps the human asks the divine One for many needs that have yet to be met. So a checklist of needs gets dumped on Him like a child sitting on Santa's lap with his wish list. Afterwards both parts having talked but not really listened to one another.

After such worship services, some people have the audacity to say, "I met with God. I know Him." Yes, they may know something *about* Him and even may have picked up a tiny, secondhand emotional lift from another person's testimony about their experience of God. But I dare say that such brief encounters do not produce real knowledge of God.

Often in worship services, the worshiper and God come no closer together; just as on airplanes strangers depart as strangers.

Flying in a plane does not make us pilots. Standing in a garage does not make us cars. And sitting in church never makes us Christians.

Knowing God requires more of us than sitting in a church. This book is your moment of truth. One critical question will be asked of you:

Do you really know God?

You will take a spiritual flight as you read the following pages. You will have many opportunities to learn about God from the pages of His book, the Bible. And periodically you can even stop and talk to God. Prayers throughout this volume can help you communicate with the One who is there and desires to talk with you.

Yet, if you read this book and simply learn something more *about* God, then its purpose has failed. My prayer is that something wonderful happens as you read—I pray that you will come to *know* God. Knowing Him means to have a relationship with Him. Yes, you can have a personal relationship with the infinite God who created the universe. That relationship will go far beyond the kind of passing acquaintances that people have on planes or even encounter in church.

This book is not about religion. Too often in churches people learn how to be religious without ever experiencing the learning that lasts. Jesus, the One who knows God most intimately among all people said this: "O righteous Father, the world hath not known thee: but I have known thee, and these have known that thou hast sent me" (John 17:25). You can be among those who know God just as He was known by Jesus.

Religion only knows *about* God. Faith through Jesus actually *knows* God. You will discover that to know God is to love Him...and to love Him is to obey Him...and to obey Him brings you into continual abiding and fellowshipping with Him...and abiding in Him produces good fruit in your life that blesses both you and all those around you.

Are you ready to know God? Don't fasten your seatbelt. Don't put your chairs and trays in an upright position. Instead, loose yourself from anything that binds, constrains, and hinders you. Move from any upright position to your knees. Humble yourself, and get ready to meet the One who created you, loves you, and desires an intimate relationship with you. Prepare not only to meet, but to know God. This flight will change your life!

*"Understanding and knowing God is
the pursuit of our lives.
Incredible benefits result from
knowing God.
That should be our pursuit."*

DAVID BLUNT

CHAPTER 1

THE GOD WE NEED TO KNOW

"Touching the Almighty, we cannot find Him out.
He is excellent."
JOB 37:23A
"Behold, God is great, and we know him not, neither can
the number of His years be searched out."
JOB 36:26

God is excellent. Excellence is not merely what God does or has, it is what He is. God is not pursuing, seeking, or becoming excellent. God is excellent.

Humanity only touches excellence in fleeting ways. It was 1976 in Montreal, Canada, that the world saw a fleeting moment of excellence and perfection. A young gymnast from Romania started her gymnastic routine on the unparallel bars. Nadia Comaneci's lithe body seemed to fly effortlessly through the exercise. As she nailed a perfect landing the crowd erupted into thunderous praise and applause. Then the judges' scores lit up the arena. Perfect 10.0 marks came from every judge. Nadia became the first person in history to record a perfect score in Olympic competition. But even that moment of glory was short–lived.

Imagine how impossible it would have been for Nadia to score perfectly in that one exercise every day for the rest of her life. Impossible, you say? Absolutely, I respond. Because humans, even when they touch excellence and perfection for a moment, cannot consistently maintain such high standards.

Humans haven't arrived yet. They still pursue excellence. In our personal lives, with our families and our churches, we strive to be the best and to be excellent. We are changing from day to day as we grow and mature in excellence. In our efforts we try to raise the standard, try to be better than yesterday's best, and try to reach a little higher than ever before. Still, true excellence is always just beyond us

God is not cheap, not average, not just okay, not mediocre, not marginal, and not approximate. God is excellent!

God never strives or tries to be excellent. *He is!* He is the standard by which all excellence is measured. Imagine the highest good, the most perfect person, the greatest power, or the purest truth. Beyond all that we can imagine or conceive is our God, who is excellent.

We desire a life of excellence because He is excellent. God lifts us beyond ourselves doing in us that which is "exceedingly abundantly above all that we ask or think, according to the power that worketh in us" (Eph. 3:30).

Going beyond our best, giving greater than any previous gift, loving more unconditionally, and forgiving without looking back are all ways we can reach for excellence. Nevertheless, our best is never good enough. To find excellence, we must *know* God.

Our God Is Great

God exists beyond our understanding and limitations. Because He is infinite and we are finite, we can neither number His days nor comprehend His ways. "For my thoughts are not your thoughts, neither are your ways my ways, saith the Lord"(Isa. 55:8).

The Hebrew understanding of *great* is not static but active, ever increasing and expanding. God's greatness is never fixed or frozen. Yes, God was great yesterday, but He is *greater* today and will be even *greater* tomorrow. God is greater than any problem or difficulty. God is greater than any hurt or guilt. God is greater than any need or dream.

In fact, just when we believe we know everything about God, we discover just how little we do know Him. God is so much greater than:

- any idea or concept we have of Him.
- any doctrine or dogma.
- any church or denomination.
- any description or definition.
- any tradition or religious creed.

Even more, He is greater than my worse fear,
my deadliest sickness,
my deepest hurt,
my blackest depression,
greater than my greatest loss.

Because God is eternal, He always knows the end from the beginning. He is Alpha and Omega. God never starts something He has not already finished. Before He creates, He knows the purpose of His creation.

Knowing that God is great and eternal is good news today. God already knows the purpose of and is greater than any problem. Since God is both great and eternal, why do you worry? How is it that you are afraid?

"Thou shalt not be afraid for the terror by night, nor the arrow that flieth by day, nor for the pestilence that walketh in darkness, nor for the destruction that wasteth at noonday. A thousand shall fall at thy side, and ten thousand at thy right hand, but it shall not come near thee" (Ps. 91:5–7). So remember, whatever you are facing: **The eternal God is greater!**

God Is Perfect

"Can you find out the deep things of God or can you by searching find out the limits of the Almighty, explore His depths, ascend to His heights, extend to His breadths and comprehend His perfection?" (Job 11:7 AMP). The New Age gurus teach that we can become little gods and attain perfection. The truth is that no one is perfect except God. He alone is fully complete, whole, and without any shadow of changing (James 1:17).

We are not God. God needs no air to breathe or food to eat. God doesn't need people. Someone said God created people because He was lonely. Wrong! God is the self–sufficient One. That simply means He has no need. God didn't need people. God doesn't need fellowship. God doesn't need praise. God never gets thirsty. God never gets hungry. God never slumbers or sleeps (Ps. 121:4).

Something else I discovered about God is that His riches are unsearchable. What does that mean? You and I can spend all our lives seeking God and never come to know all there is to know about Him. Just as some restaurants promise a bottomless cup of coffee, imagine a bottomless source of riches—no height, no breadth, no depth, being unsearchable and unreachable.

So God is perfect and unsearchable. We may ask, "Why do we live in an imperfect world?" God did not create it imperfect. God created this earth perfect. Humanity through sin made it imperfect. Sin, rebellion, pride, and imperfection are all human creations. What God made perfect, we have polluted and profaned.

Jeremiah 9:23 reveals, "Thus saith the Lord, 'Let not the wise man glory in his wisdom, neither glory in his might. Let not the rich man glory in his riches." People in the flesh pursue wisdom, power and wealth. Natural man wants what he cannot have and seeks what he does not deserve. The more possessions and power people attain, the less satisfied they are. This is like trying to satisfy one's thirst by drinking water from the sea. The more sea water we gulp, greater becomes our thirst. The Amplified Bible expands Jeremiah's warning not to seek, "earthly possessions that only have a temporary satisfaction."

Without a knowledge of God, people seek temporal things that can never satisfy. How fleeting is the glory of earthly wisdom, treasure, and might! But Jeremiah proceeds to counsel, "But let him that glorieth glory in this, that he understands and knows me."

Understanding and knowing God is the pursuit of our lives. Incredible benefits result from knowing God. That should be our pursuit. Our generation is consumed with the accumulation of stuff. We work long and hard to possess homes, cars, electronic equipment, recreational vehicles, and the like. But life is not about acquisitions.

We have come to believe the world's lie that who we are—personal identity, prestige, and status—rests in what we do and what we own. We ask, "Who am I?" However, we should be asking, "Whose am I?" For we never find meaning and purpose in our belongings. Life's purpose is rooted not in belongings but in belonging to the One we know—God.

When you know the Father, you will know His will.

We try to plan our futures and then pray that God blesses our plan. However, our first priority in life should be to know the God of the plan and then we will begin to understand the plan of God.

Too often we spend our time focusing on the will of God. That's exactly what the devil desires us to do. He distracts us from the person of God by trying to get us worrying about God's will and His plan.

Apart from His nature, you can never discover God's will apart from His nature.

I have observed Christians going from church to church, job to job, mate to mate, and career to career hoping to bump into God's will for their lives.

They become frustrated with not knowing God's will for their lives. They weep at the altar and cry through the night, "O God, show me Thy will." They do not need a revelation of God's will, they need a revelation of God! ⟵

Knowing God Transforms Us

Once we know the God of the plan of life as revealed in Scripture, then we will know the plan of God. The devil does not want us to spend time in the Word and prayer finding out more about God. Why? Because he knows that when we find out more about God, something incredible will happen in our lives. What? We will be **transformed.**

I hear people yearn to know more about the Bible but never meet the God of the Bible. I see people going to seminars on prayer but not praying to God. We are never changed and transformed by knowing more *about* God. Only by knowing God can we experience change and transformation.

We are never transformed by knowing God's plan, but we will always be transformed by knowing the God of the plan.

In this book, I pray that you will discover what to "glory in" (Jer. 9:23) throughout your life. To glory in something means to be "proud of this or that." If you are going to boast or be proud about anything, boast in the Lord. "In God we boast all the day long, and praise thy name forever. Selah." (Ps. 44:8). Jeremiah 9:24 urges us to glory in God who exercises those things in which He delights: lovingkindness, judgment, and righteousness in the earth. For in these things I delight.

One key to knowing God is delighting in those things that delight Him. As I delight myself in what pleases and delights Him, I know Him more intimately and realize more of His blessings in my life. Notice this: When I delight myself in Him, I not only know Him more intimately, but I also receive the desires of my heart. "Delight thyself also in the Lord; and he shall give thee the desires of thine heart." (Ps. 37:4).

Our prayer needs to be, "God, whatever makes you happy...God, whatever pleases you...God whatever delights you, I will spend my life being and doing." Delighting ourselves in *Him personally* and what pleases Him transforms our lives into the image of Jesus Christ.

So what delights us about God? We delight in Him not just His gifts and work in our lives. Delight comes in knowing Him and the glory of His presence in our lives. Knowing Him means to experience His excellence, greatness, and perfection. Delighting ourselves in Him becomes the basis for living life. Because God is perfect, great and excellent, we make our decisions in life based on His nature and not the flesh—which is our sin nature. The priority and desire of our hearts is to know God. Let's explore some of the desires and delights we will have in knowing Him.

To Know God Is to Experience Him

How can we know this God in whom we delight? First, our deep desire needs to be: **to experience Him.** "Oh taste and see that the Lord is good" (Ps. 34:8). Never become satisfied with the experiences that others have of God. Yes, it is a blessing to listen to the revelations and testimonies of others. But at some point, you must have a revelation. You need to have your own testimony of the goodness of God. I want you to experience the goodness of God in your own life.

"But this shall be the covenant that I will make with the House of Israel: After those days, saith the Lord, I will put my law in their inward parts, and write it in their hearts; and will be their God, and they shall be my people. And they shall teach no more every man his neighbor and every man his brother, saying, Know the Lord: for they shall all know Me: for they shall all know me from the greatest of them to the least of them, saith the Lord: for I will forgive their iniquity and remember their sin no more" (Jer. 31:33–34). God delights in our knowing Him. He desires that we become so intimate in our knowledge of Him that we will teach others to *know Him*-not just to know about Him.

The New Covenant that we experience in Jesus Christ is for the purpose of knowing God the Father. Jesus echoes the prophetic words of Jeremiah when He promises that we can know the Father through Him (John 14:7). God sent His Son Jesus that we might know Him.

When we experience God in the New Covenant, we experience His forgiveness. I know that He is a forgiving

God. There is now no condemnation for those who are in Christ Jesus (Rom. 8:1).

As a Christian if you are finding yourself constantly feeling guilty and condemned, know that you are not experiencing God but the accuser of the saints—the devil.

> *Our experience of God is not one of condemnation, but it is one of forgiveness.*

Too often I hear Christians share how battered and beaten they are, and blame God for it. Such condemnation never comes from God. If your experience of God is as an abusive, judgmental and harsh deity, then you do not know the God of Scripture. God our Father is a loving and forgiving God. "Bless the Lord, O my soul; and forget not all his benefits: who forgiveth all thine iniquities; and healeth all thy diseases" (Ps. 103:2–3).

Here is an incredible benefit of knowing and experiencing God: He forgives and forgets my sin. We shall explore the benefits of knowing God later in more depth. For now, let's discover another way we know Him so that we may receive His benefits and blessings.

To Know God Is to Trust Him

One night after church, my wife, Kim, and I had some "shopping ministry" to do at the mall. As we walked through one department store, we met another family from church that we knew were involved in "shopping ministry." So I asked them, "How are you doing?" They replied, "We are blessed!" We met another family in the mall, asked the same question, and got the same response, "We are blessed!"

Now blessing happens in the presence of God. When we trust Him, we enter into His presence and we experience His blessings. Blessing is not something we simply get from God. Blessings *flow* from knowing Him. And the only way to know Him is to trust Him.

Knowing God builds trust and faith in my life. I not only learn to trust Him but also to trust everything that He says and promises. And when I trust His promises, I experience His benefits and blessings in my life.

Let me illustrate this for you. When I do not know God, then I cannot trust what He says about tithing, giving and finances. When I don't trust His promises about finances, then I will not experience His financial blessings. If I don't know God, then I will not trust what He says about relationships. And if I don't trust His Word about my relationships, then I will never experience His incredible benefits for my marriage, my family, my children, my associates, or my friends.

As you read through this book, you will discover how to know God, and as a result of knowing God, you will grow in your trust of Him and His promises. In fact, you will be able to trust Him as never before. You will get out of your boat, your rut, and your bondage.

Imagine your car breaking down on the interstate. If someone stopped to help you, you might find it hard to trust a stranger. But if a state trooper stopped to help, you would probably trust him because you are familiar with him. Now notice that I said *probably* trust. Many church members probably trust God with some things in their lives. Why? Because they only know *about* Him.

No one can trust the unknowable.

But if a friend you had known for years stopped to assist you with a broken down car, then you would completely trust that friend. We only trust someone we know completely.

"And they that know thy name will put their trust in thee: for thou, Lord, hast not forsaken them that seek thee" (Ps. 9:10). When we know the Lord, we then trust Him and His Word.

To Know God Is to Love Him...and Others

Knowing God increases our love for Him and for others. In 1 John 4:7 we read, "Beloved, let us love one another: for love is of God; and everyone that loveth is born of God, and knoweth God." If a person cannot love others then that person cannot possibly know God because God is love. We can be certain of this one thing: that God loves people.

Now we have just seen that to know God is to trust Him. Faith in God is not expressed by volumes of right doctrine and theology. The evidence of trusting God is love. Paul writes, "The only thing that counts is faith expressing itself in love" (Gal. 5:6 NIV). We express our trust in God by love, and we love because we know Him.

The more we love people, the more involved we will be in ministry and in helping people.

One morning I took Kim out to Hardee's—I'm a big spender. As we were sitting there having breakfast, I noticed a couple that looked distraught. The lady was smoking one cigarette after another and the husband would leave, go outside, and come back in over and over again. I could tell they were worried, and they were having problems. My heart went out to them. Now, what caused my heart to go out to them? The love of God within me and knowing God cares about them.

So I had Kim begin to minister to the woman during one of the times her husband exited the restaurant. (I didn't want to talk to her and have her husband enter and see his wife talking to a stranger.) I asked Kim, "Honey, will you just go over and ask her if there is anything we can do for them?" So we spent time reaching out to them.

> *The more we will love people, the closer we get to the heart of God.*

Knowing God prompts us to love the unlovable, the untouchable, and the ungrateful. Loving will birth within us the desire to reach out to others. Children sing, "Red and yellow, black and white–they are precious in His sight." Similarly, love is more than a feeling, it's an action of compassion.

So what causes a church to reach out and help people? *Knowing God.* A church's doctrine or building will never compel us to reach out but knowing God will empower us to reach out to others. Knowing God produces rivers of love that flow from Christians into a world thirsting for love and a knowledge of God. <u>Love attracts.</u> Knowing God produces a love in us that attracts the world to Christ.

Some of the incredible benefits of knowing God include discovering that:

- God is excellent—far beyond what we can think, imagine, or do.
- God is great—greater than any circumstance or problem.
- God is perfect—completely sufficient to meet any need.
- Knowing God transforms us.
- To know Him is to trust Him.
- To know Him is to love Him and others.

Next we will discover how knowing God gives us both a foundation and direction for life. But now, for a moment, let me ask you some searching questions:

- Do you truly know God? Have you been born of God?
- Are you able to trust God with any problem or difficulty in life?
- Does love flow out of you like a river toward others?
- Have you discovered the excellent, great and perfect character of God at work in your own life?

If you answered yes to each of these inquiries then praise and thank God for the privilege of knowing Him! But if there was some doubt or hesitancy in answering any or all of these, then take a moment to pray aloud:

Almighty God, I desire to know You
more than anything else in life.
Reveal yourself to me
through Your Son Jesus Christ.
In the power of your Holy Spirit,
teach me to trust and to love.
Make of me a river of love
flowing to others that
they might know You. Amen.

CHAPTER 2

SEVEN WAYS TO KNOW GOD

"And this is life eternal, that they might know thee, the only true God, and Jesus Christ, whom thou hast sent."
JOHN 17:3

Gregg and Sharon came to me for counseling and desired to know God's plan for their lives. They had read scripture passages about the will of God, then prayed and sought the counsel of Christian friends. Both had some specific ideas about God's plan but were disagreeing with each other on what they believed about God's will for their future together. As a result, conflict and arguments arose concerning God's plan for having more children and possibly buying a larger home.

How would you have counseled this couple? In what ways should they be seeking God's plan for their lives? While both had sincere beliefs and real zeal for knowing God's will, their approach was completely wrong. They had focused all of their energy on knowing God's will and plan for their living instead of on *knowing God.* If we only focus on God's will and not on coming to know Him, then we will be frustrated, unfulfilled, unhappy, and completely without direction.

Knowing God is our first priority in life. Once we know Him, then He will reveal His plan to us. When I know the God of the plan then I will have the plan of God for my life.

Knowing God is the foundation for all of life. Knowing Him shapes our walk in the Spirit. If we know Him as a big God, then we'll walk in a big life full of abundance and prosperity. But if we know Him as a little God, then we will be beggarly, poor, and barely able to survive. When our God is too small, then we have put Him in a box that shapes our lives with limits and restrictions.

Knowing God is the goal of life. He is the direction for life. When we run life's race, He is the destination—not success, material wealth, or recognition. When we feel overwhelmed, we run to the Rock. When we battle fear and attacks of the enemy, we hide in the Rock. When spiritual bondages surround and oppress, we break them on the Rock. "Unto thee, will I cry, O Lord my rock," sings David (Ps. 28:1). When we know God, we have a rock on which to stand and a goal towards which to run. God is our rock. *our firm foundation.*

What Does God Desire?

Jesus declares that eternal life is found in knowing God (John 17:3). It is very important to Jesus that we know the Father. The importance of knowing God is also stressed in the Old Testament. "For I [God] desired mercy, and not sacrifice: and the knowledge of God more than burnt offerings" (Hos. 6:6). Before we can uncover the incredible benefits of knowing God, our first priority must be to have knowledge of Him.

Notice that sacrifice is secondary to knowing God. I know people who spend all their time in church sacrificing one thing and then another. They sacrifice time in serving God. Money is sacrificed to God. Even relationships are sacrificed in trying to please Him.

Jesus wants us to know the Father—not know about Him, but to know Him intimately and personally. When we know Him, we will understand His ways and desire His leading in our lives.

What's important to God must be important to me. When we read Colossians 1:9–10, we discover what's important to Him: "that ye might be filled with the knowledge of his will in all wisdom and spiritual understanding; that ye might walk worthy of the Lord unto all

God's desire is not our sacrifice and good deeds, rather He desires that we know Him.

pleasing, being fruitful in every good work, and increasing in the knowledge of God." Do you want to please God? Then grow in your knowledge of Him, and deepen your relationship with Him. *To do* ←

Remember, as we have said before, the Spirit of wisdom comes to us that we might know God (Eph. 1:17). Paul prays that we come to know God so that His calling, purpose, plan, and direction for our lives will be revealed.

Now be careful at this point. God doesn't want you to know Him because He needs fellowship with you. God doesn't need anyone or anything. God doesn't need people, food, air, buildings, music, money, or anything from us. He created us because He willed it. He wanted to create us. The truth is that God wants a relationship with us not because He needs it but because He simply wills it.

Just knowing God brings us into a place of incredible blessing and benefits.

Not only does God want us to get to know Him, He wants to bless us in the process. God is the source of everything. Through Jesus, the Word, God the Father created all things (Col. 1:16). So the closer we are to the Father through His Son, the more we experience all that He is. He is life, and all good gifts in life come from Him (James 1:17).

Walk with me as we look at seven awesome ways we can get to know God.

#1 — Know God Through His Son

God cannot be known apart from His Son. Jesus reveals that when we see and know Him, we know the Father, "He that hath seen me hath seen the Father" (John 14:7–9). Everything that Jesus did and said should be studied, meditated upon and lived out in our lives. His nature reveals God's nature. His actions are God's, and His Words come directly from the throne of God. He said and did nothing except what the Father wanted Him to say and do (John 8:28). So everything about Jesus shows us how to know the Father.

Imagine a huge palace you wish to tour. At the palace gate stands the gatekeeper. He is always there with the key to enter. He lives in the palace and maintains it. In fact, he built the palace to the specifications of the king. He is the king's right hand man for everything that happens in the palace. No one enters without the gatekeeper. No one comes into the presence of the king without the approval of the gatekeeper. Obviously, you must know the gatekeeper in order to know the King.

The same is true about God. To know the Father, you must know the Son who is the gatekeeper, "I am the gate: whoever enters through me shall be saved" (John 10:9, NIV).

Desire a relationship with the Father. Then know the Son. Become intimately familiar with all His Words and deeds. Learn all you can about Him through the Word. Jesus invites us, "Take my yoke upon you, and learn of me; for I am meek and lowly in heart: and ye shall find rest unto your souls" (Matt. 11:29).

#2 — Know God Through His Word

We must seek God with our whole hearts. "With my whole heart have I sought thee: O let me not wander from thy commandments. Thy word have I hid in mine heart, that I might not sin against thee" (Ps. 119:10).

Sin separates us from God. We cannot know someone intimately in a long distance relationship. Long distance relationships may last for a season, but they ultimately fade away. We need to relate face-to-face with God. We do that through knowing His Word. God related to Moses and Israel in the wilderness through His Word, the Law or Torah.

God's Word uncovers His character, describes His mighty deeds, reveals His nature, and paints a perfect portrait of His person.

Without the Word, we could never know God.

The result of knowing His Word is blessing: "Blessed are they that keep his testimonies, and that seek him with the whole heart" (Ps. 119:2). Jesus tells us that His words are Spirit and life (John 6:63). All the incredible benefits in life of knowing God are found in His Word.

#3 — Know God Through His Names

Names often reveal much about a person. In the Bible, a name like Peter means Rock and the name Abraham, means "father of nations." God used His name to reveal Himself to us. Let me share with you a brief list of the names of God in the Old Testament so that you may know something of Him:

- Yahweh or Jehovah — God is the great I AM (Ex. 4:14).
- Elohim — God is the supreme Creator (Gen. 1:1).
- Jehovah–Jireh — God is the Provider (22:14).
- SHAMMAH — God is there

- M'KADDESH - MY SANCTIFICATION
- SHALOM - MY PEACE
- El–Shaddai — God is the <u>self–sufficient</u> One who is <u>almighty</u> (Ex. 17:1). MORE than ENOUGH
- Jehovah–Rapha — God is the One that <u>healeth thee</u> (Ex. 15:26).
- Jehovah–Roi — God is <u>my shepherd</u> (Ps. 23:1).
- Adonai — God is <u>my Lord</u> (Ex. 4:10)
- NISSI - MY Banner
- TSIDKENU - MY RIGHTEOUSNESS

There are many other names, but this begins to give you an idea of how He makes Himself known through His names. Psalm 9:10 declares, "And they that know thy name will put their trust in thee: for thou, Lord, has not forsaken them that seek thee." We cannot trust the unknown.

> *Knowing God's names gives us the confidence to know and trust Him.*

Knowing that <u>God is your provider</u> helps you lean on Him instead of on your salary or job. Knowing that <u>God is your Healer</u> empowers you to seek His healing and health instead of taking a pill every time you have a headache. Seeking Him by name gives you access to His grace and marvelous benefits.

#4 — Know God Through His Attributes

Some of His attributes come to mind immediately: God is good, love, eternal, a Spirit, merciful, just, righteous, pure, and holy. And that's just a beginning. The prophet

Jeremiah speaks of His power, "Ah Lord God! behold, thou hast made the heaven and the earth by thy great power and stretched out arm, and there is nothing too hard for thee" (Jer. 32:17).

You may say, "David, you just don't understand how difficult my situation is. Yes, all of us have problems. Some have arisen because of our sins and sowing in the past to destruction. Some problems are attacks of the enemy and being persecution because we follow Jesus. And some problems arise because of the sinful world in which we live. But no problem is too hard for God. Now that is good news!

Jeremiah proceeds to reveal that "Thou showest lovingkindness unto thousands, and recompenst [compensate] the iniquity of the fathers into the bosom of their children after them: the Great, the Mighty God, the Lord of Hosts, is his name" (Jer. 32:18). We serve a great and mighty God. Jeremiah proceeds to reveal that He is great in counsel and mighty in work. That means that anything we need to know, He knows. Anything that needs to be done, He can do. When I can't, He can. He is able to accomplish whatever His will requires. His eyes are always open to see everything and to know all things. He never slumbers nor sleeps (Ps. 121:4).

You may believe that God doesn't care about your situation right now. But the truth is that He sees and cares about everything in your life. He sees every attack and every problem. God is able to overcome every obstacle and difficulty in your life. The question is: Will you come to know Him and let Him work in you?

Because God is mighty in work, we can trust that He will do awesome work in our lives and our families. "Come and see the works of God: He is terrible [awesome]" (Ps. 66:5). What is God saying to us? We serve a God who wants to do mighty works in our families, our marriages, our ministries, our jobs and in all of life. God accomplishes mighty signs, wonders, and miracles in our lives.

God wants us to come to Him and to surrender all to Him. He desires that we see His mighty works. But we can never see His works until we see His face. We can never understand His counsel until we personally know Him. Do you know God?

We serve a *big* God. Isaiah 40:12 tells us that God measures the waters in the palm of His hand and comprehends the measurements and weight of the earth. He sits on the circle of the earth and all people are as small as grasshoppers to Him (Isa. 20:22). God is really big! If you desire big things to happen in your life, get to know this *big* God of Abraham, Isaac, and Jacob.

God's awesome works will work in you if you know Him.

#5 — Know God Through Obedience

Ever known someone who claimed to know God but lived a life that violated all the principles and commands of God? Such a person may know something about God but certainly doesn't know God. We can draw close to God as we obey His Word. First John 2:1–2 states, "My little children, these things write I unto you, that ye sin not. And if any man sin, we have an advocate with the Father, Jesus Christ the righteous: and he is the propitiation for our sins: and not for ours only, but also for the sins of the whole world."

If I am in rebellion, then I am hindered from knowing God.

King Saul was unable to know God and His ways because He disobeyed God and refused to repent (1 Sam. 15).

Saul was anointed king of Israel. The Holy Spirit had come upon him empowering Him to prophesy and walk mightily with the power of God. Nonetheless, his failure to obey God brought separation and judgment on his life. Saul was unable to discern the things of God because He didn't know Him. And he didn't know God because he refused to obey Him. Those in rebellion and disobedience find themselves unable to know God. The more obedient we are to God's commands, the more we get to know Him and experience His presence, glory, and goodness in our lives.

#6 — Know God Through Praise and Worship

There is a movie, *Grumpy Old Men*. I have met some people that might be called, *Grumpy Old Church Members*. I am not speaking of being old in years but old in attitude and nature. They have never died completely to the old in their lives. They cannot praise God with joy and adoration because they are burdened by the past. They have become critical, cynical, and even bitter about some past offense or hurt. Such grumpy people cannot know the Spirit of God. How old is your attitude?

When we praise Him, we come into His presence. When we worship God, He reveals Himself to us, and we can know Him. We need to love on God and kiss the Son. Say to God right now:

> *Almighty God, You are worthy of my worship and praise. You are the eternal God, the everlasting Father. You are the Creator and the source of all things. Nothing is too hard for You. I am so thankful for all Your good gifts—family, church, job, and material blessings. Most of all, I praise You for Jesus and the gift of Your Holy Spirit. Lord, I praise and worship You. I bow down in humble adoration to You.*

Can you say that aloud to the Father? He deserves all your worship and your praise.

What keeps you from praising and worshiping Him? Look over the following list and check off anything that keeps you from worship and praise:

- Too busy.
- Too much work.
- Family problems.
- Financial worries.
- Relationship hurts.
- Past guilt and failures.
- A marriage or family crisis.
- Illness.

Whatever keeps you from worshiping and praising God will keep you from knowing Him. Set aside all distractions like busyness, financial cares, relationship problems and fears. Confess your sin and guilt. Be cleansed by the Spirit through His precious blood. Come into His presence with thanksgiving and singing. Know God through your praise and worship.

#7 — Know God Through His Creation

When did you last sit still and take the time to watch a sunrise or sunset? When was the last time you sat by the ocean or lake and watched the millions of reflected diamonds dance on the surface from a flood of sunlight or moonlight? Have you marveled at the animals in a zoo or sat mesmerized in front of an aquarium? When last did you walk through a forest bespeckled by sunlight and heard the rustle of wind in the trees? All of creation declares the glory of God (Ps. 19:1).

Natural revelation means that the creation itself points to the Creator. Let's say you were walking through a forest and discovered a watch. This mechanical device is certainly out of place in a forest. It is not alive but rather moves mechanically. By observing such an intricate mechanism, you might first conclude that it must have been made by someone—a watchmaker. You could also deduce some things about the watchmaker. For example, the watchmaker is a person of order and detail. He knows mechanics and design. No such watch could exist without a watchmaker.

So consider creation. It is filled with intricacy and detail. Its natural laws reveal a prodigious intellect behind the universe. So many marvelous laws govern creation that only a being of awesome reason and intellect could have created all that is. The apostle Paul speaks of this in Romans 1:19–20, "Because that which may be known of God is manifest in them, for God hath shown it unto them. For the invisible things of him from the creation are clearly seen, being understood by the things that are made, even his eternal power and Godhead; so that they are without excuse."

We are without excuse. All creation shouts that a Creator exists. His beauty, order, natural law, and perfect design are all revealed in creation and can be known by us.

Together we have discovered seven ways that God can be known. The Father can be known:

- through His Son.
- through His Word.
- through His names.
- through His attributes.
- through obedience.
- through praise and worship.
- through His creation.

Which way do you need to pursue right now to seek God with your whole heart? Do you hunger and thirst to know Him with all that is in you? *Yes*

In the upcoming pages, you will begin to know God as the self–existing One who is eternal. In this moment, will you seek to know Him with intensity and passion? If knowing God is your heart's desire, then pray aloud:

Almighty God,
I seek You with my whole heart.
I want to know You through Your Son;
through Your Word; through Your names;
through Your attributes; through obeying Your commands;
through praising and worshiping You; and through Your creation.
Thank you for revealing Yourself in so many wonderful
and perfect ways. Amen.

CHAPTER 3

GOD: THE SELF-EXISTING ONE

"And God said unto Moses, I AM THAT I AM: and
he said, Thus shalt thou say unto the children of Israel, I
AM hath sent me unto you."
EXODUS 3:14

What is your favorite passage of Scripture? You might choose John 3:16, or the twenty–third Psalm, the love chapter of 1 Corinthians 13 or even the Lord's prayer in Matthew 6. But what if you were asked, "What's the most *important* verse in the Bible?"

There are many important verses but all depend and spring from the foundation of just one verse—simply this: "In the beginning, God created the heaven and the earth" (Gen. 1:1). That's right. The most important verse is the first verse of the Bible. Why? Let me explain.

Without an eternal, self–existing God the rest of the Bible would make no sense. Without an eternal, self–existing God then we would have been created from stuff. You see, God existed before there was stuff, substance, or the material of creation. He created everything *ex nihilo*—out of nothing. Because He created from nothing, then we were made by His Word and breathed into by His Spirit. Impersonal stuff did not evolve us.

We were created by a personal, living God. Since He is both eternal and personal, God can be known, and we can have an eternal relationship with Him.

Knowing God means that we will discover He is the self–existing, eternal God who can be known. God is truly "there." He is the infinite–personal God, who is there and not silent. He speaks creation into being. He breathes life into us and creates us in His image. And He desires that we know Him and have a relationship with Him. God is life.

Without God there is no life...only existence.

In John 5:26 Jesus tells us that "the Father has life in himself." When God spoke creation into being through the Word, who is Jesus, we read that "In Him was life; and the life was the light of men" (John 1:4).

In Exodus 3:14, God reveals Himself: "I AM THAT I AM: and he said, Thus shalt thou say unto the children of Israel, I AM hath sent you." God is the great I AM. All life is in Him. He has no origin, no beginning and no end. He is the everlasting God who speaks all creation into being.

God further reveals His eternal nature in Isaiah 41:4, "Who hath wrought and done it, calling the generations from the beginning? I am the Lord, the first; and with the last, I am he." Then in Isaiah 44:6 God says, "I AM the first and I AM the last; and beside me there is no God." In other words, Buddha and Mohammed had a beginning and an end. They are not God.

No religion in the world reveals an eternal, infinite personal God except the biblical faith of Judaism and Christianity. No cow from India or snake from Egypt can be a god. No teacher from Tibet or yoga expert from Japan can be a god. Besides Jehovah, the great I AM, there is no god.

The Eternal God

So what is eternity? Isaiah 57:15 reads, "For thus saith the high and lofty one that inhabiteth eternity." Eternity is that which is outside of time. Eternity surrounds time. Time has a beginning and an end while eternity has no beginning and no end.

> *God inhabits eternity. He created time and space. He fills eternity.*

As the omnipresent One, He is everywhere in eternity, time, and space. God is the Alpha and Omega. He was there before the beginning and will be there for an eternity after the end.

So if you wish to hang out with the Father, accept His invitation to dwell in the high and holy place with Him—beyond the restraints of time and space and worldly things.

Listen to this exciting possibility: We can dwell with Him in that high and lofty place. How? Isaiah 57:15 reveals that those who have contrite, broken, and humble spirits can dwell with Him. God desires that we know Him as the eternal One. Psalm 90:1–2 proceeds to describe the eternal God as our dwelling place, "Lord, thou hast been our dwelling place in all generations. Before the mountains were brought forth, or ever thou hadst formed the earth and the world, even from everlasting to everlasting thou art God."

When you hang with God, you hang out in eternity because that is His dwelling place. And because He dwells in eternity, God does not change. "I said, O my God, take me not away in the midst of my days: thy years are throughout all generations... But thou art the same, and thy years shall have no end" (Ps. 102:24,27).

In eternity, God does not change. God is the same at all times. People change. The world changes. Society changes. Jobs and careers change. But God never changes. He is the same yesterday, today, and tomorrow. His Word never changes (Heb. 13:8). God is the self–sufficient and self–existent One. His moods do not change. His Word is settled for all time. He is the great stabilizer of our lives. Whenever we come truly to know Him through His Word, we discover that He is always the same, always dependable, always sure, and always there. The eternal God is outside of all boundaries—the boundaries of time, space, tradition, and human limits.

His truth is the standard for all things. What was true yesterday is true today because God is eternal. His Word and truth last forever. What He promised He will do because He is eternal and true.

We cannot box God in so that He fits our boundaries. He makes the rules.

Since an eternal God knows no limits, death cannot touch Him. God is immortal (1 Tim. 1:17). To be immortal means that He cannot die.

God is exempt from death. That means when we dwell with Him and He dwells by His Spirit in us, we will be immortal as well (1 Cor. 15). Ecclesiastes 3:11 declares, "He has set eternity in their hearts" (AMP).

When we know God through His Son, Jesus, we have eternal existence planted in our hearts. Without God, without the sense of destiny He puts in our hearts, we would only know death and hell. But in those who know Him, God has planted eternity and a knowledge of the eternal purpose and plan of God to save us through Christ Jesus.

God has planted eternity in the hearts of those who know Him.

There is a difference between eternal life and eternal existence. People in hell will have eternal existence. People on earth without Jesus just have existence but not life. We can try everything to make our existence meaningful. We might try sex, drugs, cars, wealth, campers, relationships, vocations, college, careers, degrees, and traveling. Until I know God and have eternity in my heart, I will remain unsatisfied and unfulfilled.

Without eternity in your heart, you will always be trying to keep up with the Jones', get more stuff, acquire more assets, attain more education and status, and seek more recognition from others. Only when eternity is put in your heart will you know inner peace and peace with God. Carefully ponder this verse: "He [God] has made every thing beautiful in his time. He has also set eternity in their hearts, yet they cannot fathom what God has done from the beginning to the end" (Eccl. 3:11, NIV).

Knowing that you were created for a purpose but never living it out would be like eternity without God. When a person goes to hell, they remember the life they lived on this earth. They remember the opportunities they had to know God and receive Jesus as Savior. God put eternity in our hearts, but it is our decision whether to spend it with Him or spend eternity in eternal separation-hell.

When you are witnessing to unsaved people share Ecclesiastes 3:11 with them. Let them know they were created for an eternal purpose and they must choose where they will spend eternity.

Now let's ask, "How do I receive eternal life?" If we do not want eternal existence in Hell, how do we receive eternal life? There is no life apart from God. First John 5:11 says, "And this is the record, that God hath given us eternal life, and this life is in His Son. He that hath the Son of God hath life; and he that hath not the Son of God hath not life."

In Jesus life is eternal existence. Life with God is not simply hanging around playing a harp; it is a joyous party for eternity. And God knows how to throw a party! Notice that eternal life is not in Buddha, Mohammed, Confucius, the Moons, the New Age, or crystals. Eternal life isn't found in things, rather it is found in a person-Jesus Christ.

Eternal life is not a church, a ritual or a membership. God in Christ gives us eternal life.

When we receive this precious gift from God, we also receive seven eternal benefits.

Seven Eternal Benefits From God

1. Eternal life, not eternal existence. God gives us abundant life (John 10:10) that is filled with joy, grace, mercy, love, and every good gift in the universe. We have life for eternity.

2. Eternal salvation. That means that our salvation will never end. Hebrews 5:9 declares, "And being made perfect, he [Jesus] became the author of eternal salvation unto all them that obey him." Some people believe in purgatory or some form of "waiting room" that we go to once we die. I hate waiting rooms in clinics and offices. I have actually sat for up to an hour waiting on an appointment I had scheduled months in advance. That makes me feel unimportant. Thankfully, God does not treat us like that. When the saved come home to the Father, He meets them with all the angels of heaven rejoicing.

We do not go to the grave then wait for our salvation at some point in the future. We become absent from the body and go home to be with the Lord (2 Cor. 5:1-8). From the moment you accept Jesus as Savior, your salvation is eternal!

3. Eternal redemption. I am so glad for my redemption. We were redeemed and brought out of darkness into light, out of ignorance into knowledge of God, out of death into life, and from despair into hope. We have been set free, released and redeemed from the burden of sin and guilt. The past is dead.

There's nothing to go back for and nothing in the past to shackle the present. We are redeemed from condemnation and set free to live abundant lives for Christ. "Neither by the blood of goats and calves, but by his own blood he entered in once into the holy place, having obtained eternal redemption for us" (Heb. 9:12).

God's offer of eternal redemption is truly free.

From time to time in the mail, we receive an offer from some company that looks amazing on the surface. If we go to their office and redeem the enclosed coupon (the offer reads), we will receive a free cruise, gift, or large sum of money. The truth is that redeeming that coupon is a gimmick. To receive that so-called free gift we must pay something or waste precious time listening to someone pitch a product we don't really want or need.

We cannot earn or pay for eternal redemption. No strings are attached. Paul writes, "For by grace are ye saved through faith; and that not of yourselves: it is the gift of God" (Eph. 2:8). When we redeem the blood sacrifice of Christ on the cross, we receive eternal release from sin, guilt, and death.

4. Eternal covenant. A covenant is a relationship with built-in promises. Some human covenant relationships do not last such as marriage covenants. Sadly, these covenants are broken too often today by divorce. Too many contract covenants are violated and lawsuits abound today because people have such a hard time keeping their covenants. But God never breaks His promises to us. "Now the God of peace, that brought again from the dead our Lord Jesus, that great shepherd of the sheep, through the blood of the everlasting covenant, make you perfect in every good work to do his will, working in you that which is well-pleasing in his sight, through Jesus Christ; to whom be glory for ever and ever. Amen" (Heb. 13:20).

Do you see it? God has given us an everlasting covenant, an eternal relationship with Him through Christ. You have a partnership with Him that lasts forever!

God gives us an eternal inheritance in heaven that can never be taken from us.

5. Eternal glory. In the Garden, man was crowned or clothed in glory (Ps. 8). But sin rendered humanity naked, without the garment of glory. Human life is so brief. Our decades on this planet do not begin to compare with the glory set before us in eternity with God. This life prepares us for the glory to come. "But the God of all grace, who hath called us unto his eternal glory by Christ Jesus, after that ye have suffered a while, make you perfect, stablish, strengthen, settle you" (1 Pet. 5:10).

6. Eternal inheritance. How sad it is when families fight over an inheritance. I know family members that have not spoken to one another for years because they were upset about an inheritance. I have also seen unwise children squander an inheritance in just a few years that their parents spent a lifetime accumulating. No human inheritance lasts. "And for this cause he [Jesus] is the mediator of the new testament, that by means of death, for the redemption of the transgressions that were under the first testament, they which are called might receive the promise of eternal inheritance" (Heb. 9:15). Not only are you a citizen of an eternal kingdom, you are royalty in that kingdom (1 Pet. 2:9; Exod. 19:6).

7. Eternal kingdom. God's kingdom has no end. Earthly empires come and go. To be a citizen of a nation on this planet has certain privileges and responsibilities. But changes come and go as the waves of the sea; not so with the kingdom of God. We are eternal citizens of a kingdom that has no end; therefore our benefits and privileges will never change. "But so an entrance shall be ministered unto you abundantly into the everlasting kingdom of our Lord and Savior Jesus Christ" (2 Pet. 1:11).

I know that you may be facing tremendous problems, changes, and losses in your life. No human being can promise you lasting security. No person can give you eternal benefits except Jesus Christ. He is life. He is the source of all that lasts forever. Through Him, you can meet and know the eternal God, who puts eternity in your heart.

Satan has lied to you. He may have told you that the bondage, depression, sin, and guilt you have experienced will last forever. You do not have to live with that deception. Knowing the eternal God brings eternal benefits into your life.

1. • **Eternal life** breaks the power of death over your life.

2. • **Eternal salvation** saves you from mere existence and delivers you into eternal and abundant life.

3. • **Eternal redemption** redeems and rescues from past sin and guilt washing you clean with the blood of Jesus.

4. • **Eternal covenant** gives you an everlasting relationship with God through faith in Jesus Christ who fulfills in your life every covenant promise from God.

5. • **Eternal glory** covers you with the garment of God's glory that removes all shame and clothes you with unending praise, joy, and love.

6. • **Eternal inheritance** is given to you by God so that your eternity will be filled with the riches of heaven.

7. • **Eternal kingdom** gives you citizenship in the Kingdom of God and makes you royalty.

Knowing the eternal God puts eternity in your heart that fills you with life both now and forever in Christ Jesus. If you desire to know the eternal benefits from the eternal God, then pray:

> *Eternal God, fill my heart with eternity.*
> *Bring me from mere existence into eternal life.*
> *Save me from guilt, sin, and death.*
> *Redeem me from past bondages;*
> *grant me all the promises*
> *of Your eternal covenant;*
> *clothe me with Your glory;*
> *seal in my heart Your eternal inheritance;*
> *and crown me with everlasting citizenship*
> *into Your kingdom.*
> *Through Jesus,*
> *Amen.*

CHAPTER 4

GOD: THE ALL-KNOWING ONE

> *"Dost thou know the balancings of the clouds, the*
> *wondrous works of him [God] who*
> *is perfect in knowledge."*
> JOB 37:16

I have a friend who thinks he knows it all. Often, before I can finish a sentence, he finishes it for me. No matter what the subject, he believes himself to be the expert even if he knows very little about it. Communicating with this man is very frustrating. He is a *know–it–all* who doesn't know much at all!

However, there is one with whom I love to talk. This person is the one and only know–it–all. Who is he? God, the all–knowing One. I want you to spend time and fellowship with the All–Knowing God. Only He can advise you on everything. Only He is an expert on every subject, problem, and possibility. You can trust His advice completely. He knows it all!

Let me share with you how knowing the all–knowing One will help you. First, knowing God will bring peace into your life. The turmoil and confusion you may be experiencing in an area of your life will cease. He will bring answers that will give you peace.

Second, knowing the all–knowing One will help you sort out the good ideas from the God ideas in your life. Don't be satisfied with just making good decisions—make God decisions. "In all thy ways acknowledge him, and he shall direct thy paths" (Prov. 3:6). Knowing God gives you the wisdom to make God decisions rooted in God ideas.

Finally, the all–knowing One protects us with His guiding Spirit. And where God guides, He provides. His guidance takes us on the right path, at the right time and in the right way.

Now, God knows everything that:
- did happen;
- is happening;
- could happen;
- and will happen.

God has never learned anything and never been taught anything. He knows all things. Isaiah 40:13 asks, "Who hath directed the Spirit of the Lord or being His counselor has taught Him? With whom took he counsel, and who taught him in the path of judgment, and showed to him the way of understanding?" This rhetorical question has the expected answer, "No one!"

Again the same type of question is asked by Paul in Romans 11:33, "Oh, the depth of the riches both of the wisdom and knowledge of God! How unsearchable are his judgments, and his ways past finding out! For who hath known the mind of the Lord! Or who hath been his counselor?" The same answer applies as before, "No one!"

Whatever God does is wondrous, priceless, and perfect because He is perfect in knowledge (See Job 37:16). That includes you and me. We are fearfully and wonderfully made (Psalm 139). He knows everything there is to know about you and me.

God Knows, so Ask Him!

The Bible reveals that God has perfect knowledge. "Dost thou know the balancings of the clouds, the wondrous works of him who is perfect in knowledge?" (Job 37:16). Since God knows everything past, present, and future, He knows your future and what is best for you. God knows what you need in your marriage, your job, your career, and your future decisions.

Since God knows everything, you can ask Him anything. In fact, He knows what we need and what we are about to ask before we ask. So, why do we need to ask? First, because He commanded us to ask (Matt. 18:19). You know God's private phone number given to you through the name of Jesus. In Jeremiah 33:3, God says to us, "Call unto me, and I will answer thee, and show thee great and mighty things which thou knowest not." I am so happy that His phone number isn't busy. Every child of His has a direct line to Him.

Remember, God knows everything that happened, is happening, could and will happen.

Two important truths have been revealed about the all-knowing God. First, where He guides, He provides. And second, we must ask for His provision.

Asking Him gives Him permission to act on our behalf. Often we fail to see God act because we have failed to pray and ask. Where does He need permission to act in your life right now? What keeps you from asking Him this moment for what you need? Pride? Fear? A lie from the devil? When will you ask your all-knowing Father for what you need.

We must give God permission to work in our lives.

The reason you can ask Him anytime or anyplace for what you need is that He is there. We learned that truth earlier in this book. God is the One who is there and not silent. He never leaves nor forsakes us. Even when we make wrong decisions, He stays with us (Heb. 13:5–6). When we face difficulties, God never tries or tests us with evil. Rather, God tests us with the best, with the good. You may ask, "But why does God test us when He knows where we are going?" The trials and tests are for us. They reveal to us our character and our hearts.

We mature and grow in Christian character even when we make wrong decisions. God knows the way we take and prepares us for the journey, "But he knoweth the way that I take; when he hath tried [tested] me, I shall come forth as gold" (Job 23:10)

Notice a wonderful promise in this verse, *I shall come forth*. In other words, the all–knowing God makes sure that you emerge from every trial and test as a victor, not a victim. You will not drift. You cannot drown. No person or thing can defeat you. Whatever you go through, God already knows that you will come forth.

An elderly pastor visited one of our services. After the message, he said to me, "I am better because of what I heard today. I am going to make it because of what you told me today." Please understand that this pastor had been ministering decades longer than I had. Yet the Word of God through this verse in Job gave him hope. Even when we serve God, we face times of trials and testing.

We never know all that tomorrow holds, but we know the One who holds tomorrow. So whatever you may be facing, God knows your future and promises you, "You shall come forth." You will come through it. Why? Because God knows. And He knows how to fix every problem, repair every break, and heal every hurt.

The Incredible Benefits of God Knowing You

God created you. God sees every step that you take (Job 34:21). If we walk in the right direction, He celebrates with us. If we move in the wrong direction, He doesn't leave or abandon us. He knows us and begins to direct our ways back to Him. He knows us so well that He knows every thought we think and every need we have.

Psalm 139:1 reveals, "O Lord, you have searched me, and you know me." No one knows you like God. He knows

88888888888888

888888888888

you better than your own heart, your spouse, or your parents. God knows your strengths and weaknesses, your problems and your victories. Psalm 139 proceeds to reveal that God knows our thoughts and the words we speak before we say them. How awesome is His knowledge of us! With such knowledge, He still loves us and wants the very best for us.

God's perfect knowledge of us works at all times for our benefit.

To show you what a wonderful benefit God's knowledge of us is, read carefully Psalm 56:8, "Thou tellest my wanderings..." How often we wander! I don't like my wandering moods. Do you like yours? When I wander, I tend to get lost and even hurt others and myself. I take wrong turns and run off the road. Instead of following God's pavement, I motor into the dirt roads of life and end up in ditches with flat tires finding myself going nowhere fast.

But I have discovered that because God knows my wanderings, He can take my wrong turns and turn them into triumphs. He is able to find me when I'm lost and work a wonder out of wandering. Psalm 56:8 goes on to say, "...put thou my tears back into the bottle. Are they not in thy book?" In ancient days, the mourners in biblical times would be hired by a mourning family to come and weep for the dead. They would also bring a bottle and gather up all the tears from every family member. It was their job to catch every tear from every broken heart and save them in a bottle.

Our All–Knowing God knows every tear before we shed it and has already prepared to catch each one. He shares our sorrows and comforts us in pain. He can fix and mend every broken heart. One word from God can fix your life even when you wander and weep over your losses and failures.

Not only does God know every word we will utter before we say it and every tear before we shed it, but He knows every thought before we think it. This is so important. Since He knows our thoughts before we do, He can also heal our minds from battling thoughts of insecurity and poor self–image. He can bind the destructive and pornographic thoughts we may have. Just because your mother or father had terrible thoughts doesn't mean that you have to dwell on such garbage. God knows the predisposition you may have toward thinking evil before you think it. He can shatter any strongholds in your mind and deliver your thoughts into wholeness and purity.

The God who knows your thoughts can change them if you give Him permission to act. Ask Him!

So how do we ask God and give Him permission to use all of His knowledge to change, transform, and recreate our lives? How do we tap into the knowledge of God and experience the incredible benefits of His knowledge?

1. We tap into the knowledge of God by the Spirit of God. Knowing about God doesn't change us. But allowing the knowledge of God to get into our hearts by His Spirit completely and radically transforms our lives. "Now we have received, not the spirit of the world, but the Spirit, who is God; that we might know the things that are freely given to us of God. Which things also we speak, not in the words which man's wisdom teacheth, but which the Holy Spirit teacheth, comparing spiritual things with spiritual" (2 Cor. 2:12–13). So the Holy Spirit teaches us the knowledge of God.

2. We tap into the knowledge of God through the Word of God. God's Word reveals to us His wisdom, knowledge, and understanding so that we decide on God ideas and not just good ideas. Pray that God's Word will dwell richly within you (Col. 3:16) so that you will be able to know and apply His Word in every situation of life.

3. We tap into the knowledge of God through prayer. But not just any prayer. When you do not know how to pray, let the Spirit pray through you (Rom. 8:26–28). At times you don't know anything, not even how to pray, but the Spirit knows. You can pray in the Holy Spirit and touch the deep things of God. He will reveal mysteries to you through His Spirit, answering your every need.

In knowing the all-knowing God, we have assurance and confidence that:

•Where God guides, He provides.

- He knows everything, so we can ask Him anything.
- When we ask, we give God permission to act.
- God knows that we will come forth out of every test and trial.
- God knows our thoughts before we think them and can change them before they do destruction—if we ask Him.
- Knowing our every pain and grief, God catches our tears and mends our broken hearts because He knows our every need.
- We can tap into the incredible benefits of an all-knowing God by His Spirit, by His Word and by praying in the Spirit.

If you will give permission to the all-knowing God to act in your life, will you pray:

All-knowing God,
give me God ideas not just good ideas.
Direct all my wandering back to You.
Catch my every tear and transform them into joy.
Abba Father, guide me by Your knowledge into
Your best for my life.
Amen.

CHAPTER 5

GOD: THE NEVER-CHANGING ONE

*"Every good gift and perfect gift is from above, and cometh
down from the Father of lights, with whom is no
variableness, neither shadow of turning."*
JAMES 1:17

As children we may have thought that some things
would never change. I remember going to Grandmother's house in the country. On holidays, she always prepared the same meals in the same way. Her house always had
the same smells and the furniture was always in the same
place. There were constants in her home that I thought would
never change. No matter what happened in my life, going
back to Grandmother's brought to me a sense of stability and
security. The family homeplace seemed unchanging. Of
course the day came when she had to move to a retirement
center and what I thought was unchanging did change.

While human situations will always change no matter
how stable they seem for the moment, God never changes.
He is immutable—stable, constant, and unchanging (Heb.
6:17–18).

We live in a world of rapid change. The stock market,
the economy, world politics, and even the relationships
around us swirl like whirlwinds which uproot everything and
leave massive changes in their paths. In fact, there will be

such great change in the End Times that the sun, moon and heavens will change with the final end being a new heaven and a new earth.

No matter what happens in creation or history, God is the never–changing One. James 1:17 reads, "Every good gift and every perfect gift is from above, and cometh down from the Father of lights, with whom is no variableness, neither shadow of turning." The good gifts are the natural blessings He gives and the perfect gifts are the spiritual blessings He pours out on us. Those gifts come continually because God never changes. His purpose is fixed. His will is stable. His Word is sure, and He is forever the same. God is not moody or subject to changing circumstances. He is the never–changing God.

That means we can depend on Him, His Word, and all His promises. Remember Ecclesiates 3:11 from our previous discussion? God has planted eternity in our hearts, so that we have a sense of purpose. God planted His unchanging purpose and plan in our lives. Nothing can satisfy or fulfill that purpose except God.

When we come to know God, we begin to live life and not just exist.

His eternity in us gives us an immutable, unchanging purpose and destiny. What is it? He has called us to be His children, a royal priesthood and holy nation (1 Pet. 2:9–10). Life is more than just existing month to month to work, pay bills, get up, go to sleep, eat, watch TV, and then start the cycle all over again. The unchanging God has implanted His eternity in you to empower you to live a successful, victorious Christian life.

How to Have a Successful Christian Life

In order to live victoriously, we need to know three constants that God has given us through His unchanging nature and Word.

1. We need to know where we have come from—our point of origin.
2. We need to know who we are.
3. We need to know why we are here.

The number one need we have in life is for significance. Everyone wants to feel significant and wanted. It is of supreme importance to know where we come from so that we know our significance and intrinsic worth. Scripture reveals that God created us in His image. From our inception, we have significance planted within us by God, who both creates us and shapes us to be like Him.

Since He created us, He also knows our identity. That identity comes from God being our Father and each of us freely deciding to become His children through faith in Christ. "But as many as received him, to them gave he power to become the sons of God, even to them that believe on his name" (John 1:12).

Why are we here?

The eternal purpose for all of God's children was declared by Christ, "Thou shalt worship the Lord thy God, and him only shalt thou serve" (Matt. 4:10) and "Thou shalt love the Lord thy God with all thy heart, and with all thy soul, and with all thy mind. This is the first and great commandment. And the second is like unto it, Thou shalt love thy neighbor as thyself. On these two commandment hang all the law and the prophets" (Matt. 22:37–39).

Nothing has changed about where we come from, who we are, and why we are here. God is unchanging and so is His plan and purpose for our lives. Psalm 102 states, "They [creation] shall perish, but thou shalt endure: yea, all of them shall wax old like a garment; as a vesture shalt thou change them, and they shall be changed: But thou art the same, and thy years shall have no end" (vv. 26–27). God does not do bad things to good people. Every good and perfect gift comes from Him.

God's purpose and plan for us was good.

So if He is unchanging why is there such suffering and evil when He created everything to be good (Gen. 1:31)? Evil exists not because of God but because of sin. We brought sin into the world.

Before humanity sinned against God in the garden (Gen. 2–3), there was no sickness, no cancer, no violent storms, no famine, no earthquakes, no child abuse, no murder, no pain, and no suffering.

But because of our disobedience, He allowed a curse to come upon creation. Through our free will and choice, we brought sin and suffering into the world. We suffer as a consequence of all the sinful generations that have gone before us. As a result of our own sin and the sin of those around us, we must contend with the world and the flesh daily.

Even though there is sin and evil, God has not changed. He is the same. God is the source and giver of every good and perfect gift. Are you looking for the author, creator, and finisher of evil? Then don't look at God. Look in the mirror. Look at the world around you. Look at the millenia of sin humanity has dumped on the world through countless acts of violence, war, abuse, slavery, injustice, and pollution.

Your confidence in God and in His identity and calling for you will expand as you know God.

The good news is that God never changes but we can change. Praise God! The never–changing God can change us through the power of the Holy Spirit. We change but He doesn't. So we can return to what is unchanging—good and perfect—which has always been and will always be in God.

There are four unchanging attributes that you need to know about God. As you grow in your knowledge and understanding of these qualities of God's nature, your level and trust in God will also increase. We cannot trust the unknown.

#1 — God Never Changes His Character

The nature and personality of God never changes. Unlike us, His moods do not change and His feelings remain constant. For example, He loves you just as much today as the day you were saved. You may have been born again years ago, but He loved you infinitely then and He loves you infinitely now. But, David, you say, I am living a much holier and more righteous life now. That's because of God working in and through you. But remember, His love isn't earned or doesn't increase because you are growing, learning and being sanctified. His unconditional love and grace are unmerited and undeserved. We simply receive the love He freely gives in Christ Jesus.

Malachi 3:6 reveals, "You see, I am the Lord and I change not." But what about the places in the Bible where it says that God repented. In those passages, the word *repent* refers to God changing His mind, not His character. God changes His mind in response to our changing our minds. But God will never change His character. As godly parents, we may change our minds in response to the behavior and obedience of our children, but we should never change our love and care for them. God's character never changes.

#2 — God's Word Never Changes

God has fixed His purpose and will which He reveals in His Word. Psalm 119:89 reads, "Forever, O Lord, Thy Word is settled in heaven." You may have heard the saying, "God said it. That settles it. I believe it." God's Word is settled whether I believe it or not. I have heard people say, "Well, I know the Bible says such and such, but I don't know if it's right or if I believe it." It does not matter whether we believe the Word or not. God's Word is always unchanging and right.

His Word is a rock and solid foundation. God never makes a promise and then retracts it. There are over seven thousand promises in the Bible. All are true and unchanging. Paul writes, "They [God's promises] are yea and Amen in Christ Jesus" (2 Cor. 1:20).

God has and will keep every promise in His Word. His Word is unchanging.

#3 — God Never Changes His Purpose

I remember building a house and talking with the contractor. He warned us that we must be decisive at the beginning of our plans. Once the plans were drawn and accepted for our home we could not change our plans without such changes being very expensive. Human beings change plans and purpose quite often much to the dismay of others and God. But God never changes His plan or purpose. Isaiah 14:24 clearly describes this: "The Lord of hosts hath sworn, saying, Surely as I have thought, so shall it come to pass; and as I have purposed, so shall it stand."

Some teach about varying degrees of God's will for our lives. We know without a shadow of a doubt that God's *perfect* will for us is to be saved and then sanctified totally through Christ. God's desire is that all be saved (1 Tim. 2:4). Once we are in His perfect will, He does allow us His *permissive* and *acceptable* will. Some things God permits and accepts in our lives, but He works only His perfect will in us. He has a plan and purpose for the lives of saints and nothing changes that. He purposes for His body, the church, to make disciples of the lost and to lift up Jesus in all worship and service. He plans to rapture the Church away to glory in His timing. Nothing is going to change that plan.

God is a planner. He not only shows you the plan and purpose for your life, but He also gives you the power and strength to do what He wills. What God plans and purposes happens. His purpose never changes.

#4 — God's Attributes Never Change

Think for a moment of all of God's qualities and attributes: His truth, love, mercy, faithfulness, holiness, justice, righteousness, lovingkindness, grace, long–suffering, patience, forgiveness, judgment, wisdom, power, and glory—just to mention a few. In the Amplified Bible we read, "Accordingly God also in His desire to show more convincingly and beyond doubt, to those who were to inherit the promise, the unchangeableness of His purpose and plan, intervened (mediated) with an oath. This was so that by two unchangeable things [His promise and His oath], in which it is impossible for God ever to prove false or deceive us, we who have fled [to Him] for refuge might have mighty indwelling

I am doing just as God said because He cannot lie.

strength and strong encouragement to grasp and hold fast the hope appointed for us and set before [us]" (Heb. 6:17–18).

It is impossible for God to lie (Num. 23:19). God hides nothing from us that we need to know about Him and His plan. We live in a world that is full of hidden agendas and self-seeking people. But God Himself has sworn an oath and made a promise never to lie and never to change His Word.

Now notice this. Preacher, teachers, prophets and evangelists may lie to me but God will not. He promised me eternal life and His love forever. And I know that He cannot lie. He told me to trust Him and seek heaven—not trust the devil—and be certain to shun Hell.

God is truth. In other words, every attribute of God is unchanging, and I can trust everything about Him. I can trust Him in life and in death; with my family and my friends; in good times and bad times; in sickness and in health. In other words, God's attributes never change, and He can be trusted.

Having affirmed that, let's look at four things that cannot be trusted:

1. Don't trust yourself. That's right. We cannot trust ourselves. We can have no confidence in the flesh (Phil. 3:3). We cannot trust our feelings, our thoughts, or our hearts. I've heard so many people in ignorance say, "Oh, just go with your heart," or "Trust your gut feeling." No way! There will be times when you don't feel saved, but the Word of God says you are.

Trust the Word not your feelings.

2. Don't put your trust in those around you. Yes, at times we must trust others. But if we put all of our trust in human beings, we will soon face disaster. Everyone, even a close friend or loving spouse, will violate our trust at one time or another. Psalm 146:3 warns, "Put not your trust in princes, nor in the son of man, in whom there is no help." The government, our employers, and social organizations or institutions cannot be trusted to fulfill all their promises and to seek only the best for us. Only God wants all the best for us all the time and is able to accomplish the best whenever He wills.

You may have changed, but He never changes.

3. Don't trust in *things*. Some put their futures and their trust in the stock market, bonds, savings, real estate, gold, or other assets. But we can lose things as quickly as we might acquire them. Psalm 20:7 advises, "Some trust in chariots, and some in horses; but we will remember the name [or the character] of the Lord our God." All material things can be corrupted, lost or stolen. Our only security is God.

1. Refuse to trust man–made systems or inventions. I see so many sick people completely trust the health care system, doctors, or the sophisticated equipment and technology we have today to diagnose and treat disease. Praise God for all of these wonderful inventions, but these things come and go. The moment an invention is conceived it becomes obsolete. All our technology with computers, electronics, and mechanical devices will change and eventually pass away. Only God remains unchanging.

Psalm 9:9 answers the question about whom to trust, "The Lord also will be a refuge for the oppressed." Satan is the oppressor and Jesus is the deliverer. Sin puts us in bondage but Jesus sets us free. Don't give in or give up. Don't let go of God. Don't lose hope. Don't let your dreams be shattered. Run to God. Though you may have turned away you can always return again.

Remember the parable of the loving Father which we often call the parable of the prodigal son? (Luke 15:11–32) The son took what he believed to be a sure and lasting thing—his financial inheritance—and left the father. In a foreign land, he put his trust in new friends who stayed with him only while the money lasted. Out of money and deserted by friends, this son ended up losing everything—feeding and eating with

If God seems distant from you, guess who has moved?

pigs. Everything he thought was certain had changed. But then he "came to his senses." He remembered how unchanging things were back at home with his father. Even there the servants were treated well.

So the prodigal son made his way back home. Nothing had changed with the heavenly Father. He still loved His son and daily looked down the road to see if His son might be returning. One day in the distance, the Father spotted His son, ran to him, embraced him and welcomed the son home.

In the son's life everything had changed except one reality—the love of His Father for him.

If everything and everyone around you seems to be changing for the worse, guess who remains steadfast in goodness and desiring your best? God! He is the never-changing One who is always there for us.

Your trouble is not terminable. Your way is not hopelessly lost. Your trust can be restored and your future can become certain. Put your trust in the God in whom there is no shadow of turning.

Together we have discovered that the way:

- to have a successful life is to know God so that our level of trust in Him can increase.
- to be confident in God is to know that God never changes His character, Word, purpose, or attributes.
- to trust Him completely is not to put our trust in ourselves, others, things, or man–made inventions or devices.
- to find security, refuge, and restoration is to turn to the God who never changes.

Each of the above ways is an incredible benefit that comes from knowing God. Knowing Him increases our faith, trust, confidence and sense of security for the present and future.

Is the ground that you trust beneath you shaking with the earthquakes of broken promises and relationships? Have you discovered that the stuff you thought you owned can never be kept secure? Do you know the God who never changes as your sure rock, refuge, and foundation?

To affirm or reaffirm your absolute trust in the unchanging God, then pray:

O God who never changes,
be my anchor in the storms,
my refuge from the attacks,
my hope when floods of despair rush in,
and my standard for every decision.
And God, immutable and unchanging,
I put my absolute trust in You—
trusting Your character, Word, purpose, and attributes.
For I know that You and You alone will be there
whenever, however, and wherever I need You.
Amen.

CHAPTER 6

GOD: THE ALL-POWERFUL ONE

"And when Abram was ninety years old and nine, the Lord appeared to Abram, and said unto him, I am Almighty God; walk before me, and be thou perfect."
GENESIS 17:1

Small children believe their dads to be invincible. When a small boy is intimidated by the playground bully, he often invokes the name of his father to scare his attacker away. "If you don't leave me alone, I'll tell my dad, and he'll beat you up," warns the overmatched child trembling all over but keeping a stiff upper lip. Now if the bully has ever felt the anger of that kid's dad, he will back off. But some bullies are stupid, just like Satan. They try to attack only to face in that moment the towering figure of Dad standing behind his child and ready to put any would be attacker to flight.

An omnipotent, all–powerful God stands behind you ready to put any enemy to flight and to defeat any attack from evil. Note how powerful this God is: "And I heard as it were the voice of a great multitude, and as the voice of many waters, and as the voice of mighty thunderings, saying, Alleluia! For the Lord God omnipotent reigneth" (Rev. 19:6). We need to know that our God reigns. He is all–powerful and all–strength. God does not increase or decrease in power. All power resides in Him. He has the power to fulfill all His promises and to accomplish His purpose and plan in your life.

Jesus declares that "with God nothing is impossible" (Matt. 19:26). That means that God and I make a majority. Possibility thinkers are those who go with God and not with man. Jesus adds in Luke 18:27 that "the things that are impossible with men are possible with God." I choose to move in the supernatural realm of the possible with the all–powerful God. Do you?

All things are possible to him who believes and trusts God. The Word does not promise the impossible to those who have large bank accounts, high intelligence or great athletic ability. The impossible is promised to believers: "All things are possible to him who believes" (Mark 9:23). So I choose to be a believer and not a doubter. If you were to go to God's Dictionary and look for the word *impossible*, you would be surprised. That word isn't there.

"Impossible" is not in the vocabulary of God.

When Abram was ninety–nine years old God appeared to him and made both a covenant and a promise to him (Gen. 12:1–3; 17:1–3). God stated, "I am the Almighty God (El–Shaddai)." As God Almighty, He promised Abram a son in his old age and a nation as his descendants. For Abram and Sarai to have children in their nineties was only possible through an all–powerful God. Only El–Shaddai can author the impossible.

So if you want the miracle–working power of God in your life, what must your heart be like?

1. **Walk blameless before God with an upright heart (Prov. 11:20).** God is looking for people of integrity to walk before Him. Paul writes in 1 Thessalonians 4:3–4 that those being sanctified by God's Spirit should abstain from immorality and become vessels of honor who never defraud or deal dishonestly with others. We need people of truth and integrity for God to use in mighty ways.

2. **We need to seek God wholeheartedly.** Psalm 119:10 describes how we should seek God, "With my whole heart have I sought thee." We fix our hearts on God. We desire all that He desires. We obey all that He says. And we follow Him wherever He leads. Some say that they have never experienced the power of God in their lives. They need first to have integrity and then seek God with their whole hearts.

3. **When our hearts are wounded, they stay right with God.** In other words, a heart seeking God's power doesn't allow offenses to block the power. If a hurt arises, so does forgiveness. If pain happens, the wounded heart seeks the power of God to take care of the hurt. Before God can touch us with His power in worship, we must be reconciled with those who hurt us and have healed hearts (Matt. 5:21–26).

Demonstrations of God's Power

God demonstrates His power through creation. "Ah, Lord God! Behold, thou hast made the heaven and the earth by thy great power and stretched out arm, and there is nothing too hard for thee" (Jer. 32:17). Because He is almighty, nothing is too difficult for God. We sing a chorus called, "What a Mighty God We Serve." That is so true. He is a mighty God, great in counsel, and mighty in work (Jer. 32:19). God is able when we are unable. God accomplishes when we fail. God has power when we are powerless. And God possesses abundant strength even when we are weak.

Our weaknesses are simply God's opportunity to demonstrate His power.

God also demonstrates His power through the spoken Word. God upholds creation through His Word. "Who [Jesus], being the brightness of his glory, and express image of his person, and upholding all things by the word of his power, when he had by himself purged our sins, sat down on the right hand of the Majesty on high" (Heb. 1:3). So by His Word God sustains all of creation including us.

Finally God demonstrates His power in keeping us safe. "According as his divine power hath given unto us all things that pertain unto life and godliness, through the knowledge of him that hath called us to glory and virtue" (2 Pet. 1:3). Through Jesus' redemption of us on the cross, God demonstrated His power to save us from death to life. His power extends to protecting you daily from sin and the attacks of the enemy. As awesome as the demonstrations of God's power are, we only witness the fringes of His power. The whole chapter of Job 39 asserts the omnipotence of God, and Job 26:14 affirms, "Lo, these are parts of his ways; but how little a portion is heard of him! But the thunder of His power, who can understand?"

God's might far exceeds our ability to understand or comprehend. But we do not have to understand God's power to experience it. We simply need to yield, to trust, and to know Him.

Nothing and No One Is More Powerful Than God

I become so weary of people talking about how powerful the devil is. He is not powerful at all compared to God. He only has power when we let him take it. Psalm 89:6–8 declares, "For who in the heavens shall praise thy wonders, O Lord; thy faithfulness also in the congregation of the saints. For who in the heavens can be compared unto the Lord? Who among the sons of the mighty can be likened unto the Lord?" No one compares to the mighty One that you and I serve. He is El Shaddai, the God who is always more than enough to meet any need and overcome any adversary.

If you own a very powerful machine that required electricity but did not know anything about it, that machine would be worthless. Likewise, to know about God's power but not to know Him is useless to you. You must know God in order for His power to be at work in your life. Psalm 135:4–5 states, "For I know that the Lord is great, and that our Lord is above all gods." God's people are destroyed for a lack of knowledge.

If I really know God and am intimately acquainted with His ways, then no circumstance can depress me. No devil or demon can oppress me. No human enemy can overcome me. And no attack from any source will ever have victory in my life. For I *know* that my God is powerful and *greater than* anyone or anything else in the universe. He that is in me is greater than he that is in the world (1 John 4:4). Whatever pleases Him to do in my life and through my life He can do: "Whatsoever the Lord pleased, that did he in heaven, and in earth, in the seas and all the deep places" (Ps. 135:6).

Knowing God unlocks His power for your life.

Are you allowing God to act in power in your life doing *whatever He pleases?* Have you grown beyond asking Him to do whatever you please to doing whatever He pleases? Surrendered and obedient, you can become a powerful instrument for the gospel in the hands of almighty God. Let almighty God do whatever He pleases in your life.

Four Things God Cannot Do

There are some things that God cannot do.

- God cannot lie (Heb. 6:17–18). He is truth and will never deceive us.
- God cannot deny Himself (2 Tim. 2:13). Whatever God has promised, He will do. God never breaks His promises.
- God cannot sin or err (Isa. 6:3). God is holy and perfect.
- God cannot act contrary to His nature (James 1:17). He will always be Himself. God cannot and does not change. He can change His mind but not His nature.

Anything that is outside of God's nature, He will not do. I have heard jokers and mockers ask, "Well if God is so great, can He make a rock so large that He cannot pick it up?" No. God doesn't do dumb, stupid, or ignorant things. All things are possible in His power, but He never does anything outside of His nature. God doesn't put sickness on people. God never authors evil. God is good and will never use His power for evil.

God Will Give Us Power

In sin, we are powerless (Rom. 5:6). The one overwhelming reality that we must face when considering God's power is just how weak and powerless we really are. We are not tough dudes. We have no strength in us to overcome temptation, sin and death. We must face the truth: we are weak!

The gospel is that He is strong. Though we are weak, He will give us strength. "The Lord will give strength unto his people; the Lord will bless his people with peace" (Ps. 29:11). So what kind of strength does He give us?

God's strength is *unyielding*. He gives us stubborn strength. He gives power and strength that will not give in, give up, give out, or go back.

One of the greatest temptations you will face as a Christian is *wanting to quit*. Too many couples, when faced with tough circumstances, are tempted to quit in their marriages. Too many workers when things are tough at the job desire to quit. Many saints when witnessing to a lost family member or friend are tempted to quit.

God gives us the strength not to quit.
God is giving us unyielding strength. His power in us will not quit when we are facing giants, going through disappointments or experiencing evil, pain and hurt. Remember that the devil cannot take you down as long as you allow God's strength in you to do whatever He pleases with your life.

Another word that describes God's strength is *impenetrable*. When the fiery darts of the evil one start flying your way (Eph. 6:16), His power in your life surrounds you with an impenetrable shield. God's power at work in you is both *unyielding* and *impenetrable*. No evil one or thing can touch you. "There shall no evil befall thee, neither shall any plague come nigh thy dwelling. For he [God] shall give his angels charge over thee, to keep thee in all thy ways" (Ps. 91:10–11). Now that is unyielding and impenetrable power!

God has promised us His power. And He always keeps His promises. In Luke 24:49, Jesus promises that if His disciples would wait in Jerusalem that they would receive power. That power came upon the believers at Pentecost (Acts 1–2) and is available to us to this day.

In Ephesians 1:15–23, Paul prays that God's people will receive the "exceeding greatness of his mighty power toward us who believe, according to the working of his mighty power." God's exceedingly great power is available to all who believe in Him. Those who have surrendered their lives to Christ, who trust Him and therefore know Him, are filled with the exceedingly great power of God.

God's power is for believers, not doubters, pouters, murmurers, grumblers, mockers and skeptics.

Make a decision now to believe in Christ. Nothing is too hard for Him. Know God through Christ Jesus and receive His wonder–working power.

Remember that seeking to know God with your whole heart releases His power in your life:

- To do whatever pleases Him.
- To overcome any circumstance in life.
- To be unyielding and able to resist any temptation to quit.

- To have His impenetrable power to quench every fiery dart of the wicked one.
- To do the impossible.
- To move and act in the realm of the supernatural power of the possible.

An incredible benefit of knowing God is experiencing His power in our lives. By His power we move into the benefits of living in the supernatural.

Pray for the power of almighty God to work within you now:

Lord, I believe and trust in You.
I desire with my whole heart
that You do in my life whatever pleases You.
I seek to know You
and the exceeding greatness of Your power
working in me to overcome every sin,
temptation and desire to quit in my life.
Amen.

CHAPTER 7

GOD: THE FAITHFUL ONE

"O Lord, thou art my God; I will exalt thee, I will praise
thy name; for thou hast done wonderful things; thy counsels
of old are faithfulness and truth."
ISAIAH 25:1

When a parent promises to do something with a child, great disappointment arises if that parent is unfaithful and breaks his promise. Occasionally, parents will break a promise and must ask a child to forgive them. But God always keeps His promises. He is loyal, faithful, and true to us according to His word.

Whatever God speaks to us is faithful and true. When God has promised you something and hope springs up in your heart, don't let the devil rob you of your expectations in God with his lies and deceptions. Lamentations 3:21–23 promises, "This I recall to my mind; therefore have I hope. It is because of the Lord's mercies that we are not consumed, because his compassions fail not. They are new every morning; great is thy faithfulness."

God has good things planned for you (Jer. 29:10–13). What He has promised and planned for you, it will come to pass. Stand firm in your faith and see God's faithfulness. We may waver and break our promises but God never does. He is reliable, dependable, stable, consistent, and sure. There is no one like our God. He never lies.

Make this the cry of your heart today: "Hear my prayer, O Lord, give ear to my supplications. In your faithfulness answer me and in your righteousness" (Ps. 143:1, AMP). Why? Because you can count on God to be faithful not only today but always (Ps. 146:6). So whenever you cry out to Him, God is there to hear your prayers and faithfully answer you according to His Word.

I want to share with you five keys to life that will unlock the faithfulness of God in your life. After the first key of knowing God, each subsequent key is an incredible benefit resulting from knowing God.

Five Keys to Experiencing God's Faithfulness

Key 1: Knowing God. We cannot know His faithfulness until we know Him. As we have discussed, knowing God involves seeking and trusting Him wholeheartedly. Paul prays in Colossians 1:9 that we increase in our knowledge of God. Are you praying to increase in knowing Him?

Key 2: Loving God. As our knowledge of God increases, so does our love. Going through the motions at church and in our daily lives of trying to live for God is not enough. As we grow in our knowledge of Him and His attributes and characteristics, we discover that knowledge creates a love for God. We cannot love one we do not know. If you are having a hard time loving God, then get to know Him. If you make a quest to know Him, you will begin to love Him passionately and deeply. Love Him with your whole heart, mind, soul and strength (Matt. 22:37).

Key 3: Obey God. As we begin to know and love God, our heart's desire is to obey Him. Knowing God brings me to loving Him. Loving Him creates a desire to obey Him. We obey God out of love and not duty. Jesus tells us, "Ye are my friends, if ye do whatsoever I command you" (John 15:14).

Key #4: Fellowship with God. As you are obeying God, you discover that you are spending more and more time with Him and His Word. Obedience births the blessing of fellowshipping with Him. I find it difficult some nights to go to sleep. I love reading the Word, praying, and fellowshipping with Him. Fellowship is better than television, radio, and the stereo. Our fellowship with the Father (1 John 1:3) is so precious that we will not let anything in the world interfere with it.

In knowing Him, you love Him. In loving Him, you obey Him. In obeying Him, you abide in fellowship with Him.

So your relationship grows from knowing to loving; from loving to obeying; and from obeying to fellowshipping with God. So what is the end result of this relationship? Here's the final key to life in Christ.

Key #5: Being fruitful for God. In reading John 15, it becomes most evident that the end result of abiding in Christ is bearing fruit. "In this is my Father glorified, that ye bear much fruit, so shall ye be my disciples" (John 15:8).

In Luke 5:3, Jesus asks Peter to "thrust out a little from the land." Many people want to launch out into the deep waters before they are faithful with just a small step. As we get to know God, we begin to love Him more and more. Then our love creates within us a desire to obey Him and in obeying we begin to abide in His presence. As we fellowship with Him, the Lord begins to test us. He gives us little things to do that will bear good fruit.

God may be saying to you right now, "Get involved just a little in working at church." Just show up. Just worship, sing, clap, raise your hands, and pray. Just tithe and serve in ministry. Some people feel that as soon as they begin to know just a little of God, they have to rush into full-time ministry and do big things for God.

Then Jesus commands Simon in Luke 5:4, "Launch into the deep and let down your nets for a draught." If you and I would just give God a little, and be faithful and fruitful in the small things, then God who is faithful will bring a harvest of fruitfulness that we cannot contain. After Peter does the little things, he then launches into the deep water and experiences the fullness of God.

We will never know God in the deep things of the Spirit until we know Him first in the little things. We will not experience God's faithfulness in healing cancer until we know Him to be a healer of our headaches and colds. Peter had been faithful in small things and had experienced Jesus' faithfulness to him. But now, Peter was launching into deep waters. There he experienced the net–breaking, boat–sinking, miracle–working power of God. God is faithful. You can trust and step out on His Word because He is faithful.

The first step in bearing fruit is to be faithful in a little.

Whatever fruit God produces in your life is for others. Whatever God does in your life, He does it so that you can share with others. So let's see this very simply:

- To know God is to love Him.
- To love God is to obey Him.
- To obey God is to fellowship with and abide in Him.
- To abide in God produces fruitfulness in our lives.

God Is Like...

We know that God will produce good fruit in our lives because He is faithful. How do we experience His faithfulness? What is the faithfulness of God like?

- God is like a coke. He's the real thing.
- God is like General Electric. He lights up your path.

- God is like Bayer Aspirin. He works wonders.
- God is like Hallmark cards. He cares enough to send you the very best.
- God is like Tide detergent. He gets the stains out others leave behind.
- God is like VO5 hairspray. He holds through all kinds of weather.
- God is like Dial soap. He cleans you through and through.
- God is like Sears. He has everything.
- God is like Alka–Seltzer. Try Him, you'll like Him.
- God is like Scotch tape. You can't see Him but you know He's there.
- God is like American Express. You can't leave home without Him.

God is abundantly faithful for his mercies are new every morning (Lam. 3:22). He gives us a new song in the morning (Ps. 9:16). God gives joy in the morning (Ps. 30:5) and we hear His lovingkindness in the morning (Ps. 143:8). Our prayer needs to be, "Lord, cause me to lean on your faithfulness every morning. Do a new thing in me each morning. I desire your new mercies, lovingkindness, songs, joy, and love each new day."

Are you ready to experience God's faithfulness anew each and every morning? Do you want each day to be filled with knowing God, loving Him, obeying His Word, abiding in Him, and bearing His fruit? Then ask Him. He is faithful to answer your prayer and draw close to you. You can trust Him to be faithful to you each day.

The Faithfulness of God Is...

No person can keep his promises or be faithful to you like God can. Everyone will fail you at one time or another. In fact, you cannot be faithful to yourself. Remember all those New Year's resolutions you made in the past. How many of them are you still keeping? No one is faithful like God. Here are six characteristics of His faithfulness that you can trust daily:

1. God's faithfulness is everlasting (Ps. 119:90). Tomorrow, next month, next year and decades from now, God will be faithful. He will never fail you.

2. God's faithfulness is established (Ps. 89:2). He is stable, secure and steadfast. You can stake your life on His faithfulness.

3. God's faithfulness is unfailing (Ps. 89:33). Yes, others will fail you. Stuff will fail you. You will even fail to keep promises made to yourself. But He will never fail you.

4. God's faithfulness is infinite (Ps. 36:5). You cannot exhaust His faithfulness. God's faithfulness is not like gasoline in your car. After so much is used, the tank is empty and you need a refill. But God has an endless supply of faithfulness for you.

5. God's faithfulness is great and abundant (Lam. 3:23). He has enough faithfulness to keep His promises to you anytime, anywhere and anyway.

Because He is faithful, you can stop fretting. Psalm 37:1 says, "Fret not thyself because of evildoers, neither be thou envious against the workers of iniquity." Stop worrying. And be careful about what you say. Some people are always saying, "I'm worried that...." You become what you say. You believe what you say. And then you receive what you believe. So fret not and don't speak any anxiety. God is faithful to care for you.

Feed on His faithfulness. What replaces worry? Psalm 37:4 gives the answer, "Trust in the Lord, and do good; so shalt thou dwell in the land, and verily thou shalt be fed." Replace worry with feeding on God's faithfulness. How? We go through the Bible studying the Word of God. We feed our spirits with the Word of God—spiritual food. Worry is junk food for your life. The Word gives real food and substance. Feed on His faithfulness each morning, not on your worry.

Praise God for His faithfulness. Not only can we feed on His faithfulness, we can praise Him for His faithfulness (Ps. 100). We know that He will be faithful tomorrow even before tomorrow comes. And we need to acknowledge and recognize that God is faithful. Deuteronomy 7:9 commands us, "Know, therefore, that the Lord thy God, he is God, the faithful God, who keepeth covenant and mercy with them who love him and keep his commandments to a thousand generations." God is in covenant relationship with us. He faithfully keeps His covenant with His people.

So we recognize and acknowledge the faithfulness of God. In Deuteronomy 7:9, we are commanded to know that He is faithful. Knowing God reveals that He can always be trusted and His Word is always true.

Faithfulness: We feed on it, praise Him for it, recognize and acknowledge it, and finally trust His faithfulness.

Trust God's faithfulness. "I will sing of the mercies of the Lord forever; with my mouth will I make known thy faithfulness to all generations" (Ps. 89:1). Too often we use our mouths to confess our anxieties instead of proclaiming His faithfulness.

If all I speak is worry, I will become anxious and doubtful. The important thing is for God's people to declare His faithfulness. Once we begin declaring His faithfulness, we will act upon what we have declared. Speak often and to everyone about the faithfulness of God.

> *What I say with my mouth long enough, I will believe and receive.*

Are you speaking of His faithfulness or your failure? Are you trusting His promises or your weak resolutions? Do you praise Him for what He will do or worry about what others might do to you? Have you committed all to trusting His faithfulness?

Psalm 84:12 tells us, "O Lord of hosts, blessed is the man who trusteth in thee." We can trust God because He alone is faithful. In whom do you put your commitment and trust?

We have discovered that there are five keys to a deep relationship of knowing God:

1. Knowledge
2. Love

3. Obedience
4. Fellowship (Abiding)
5. Fruitfulness

And we have uncovered five characteristics of God's faithfulness. His faithfulness is:

1. Everlasting
2. Established
3. Unfailing
4. Infinite
5. Great (Abundant)

So in order to experience the incredible benefits of knowing God's faithfulness to keep His covenant with us, we must:

•Feed on His faithfulness.
•Praise His faithfulness.
•Acknowledge His faithfulness.
•Trust His faithfulness.
•Declare and speak His faithfulness.

Trust His faithfulness and pray:

Lord, You are faithful in all things.
By Your Spirit, help me to know You
so that I might love You,
and in loving you I might obey You,
and in obeying you I might abide in You
and be fruitful.
Lord, I declare that You are faithful.
Amen.

CHAPTER 8

GOD: THE ONE WHO IS JUST AND GOOD

"And I heard the angel of the waters say, Thou art righteous, O Lord, who art, and wast, and shalt be, because thou hast judged thus."

REVELATION 16:5

One Saturday night on my way home from church with my son Daniel, something caught my eye just before I turned off the road toward our home. It looked like a person in light clothing stumbling along the side of the road.

I asked Daniel if he had seen someone but he hadn't. Still I knew I had seen someone hurting. We turned around, drove back down the road, and we saw her—a young lady possibly in her twenties stumbling along the side of the road. I didn't know if she was high, drunk, or if she had been beaten, stabbed, or shot. As we slowly drove back, suddenly there she was having fallen and now lying in front of us on the road.

I stopped the car and said, "Daniel stay here and let me get out of the car and see what the problem is." So I got out of the car and walked up slowly because I didn't know what the situation was.

"Are you all right?" I asked her.

She wouldn't answer me. I got a little closer holding my hand out saying, "Can I help you? Are you OK?"

Suddenly she lifted up her head and exclaimed, "Why didn't you run over me?"

I was stunned. Then she went on to say, "I want to die. I'm laying here to die. Why wouldn't you run over me? Why did you stop?"

Life had been unfair for this woman, and she wanted to die. She was laying there on the road hoping someone would run over her and kill her. She looked up at me and she said, "Why didn't you run over me? Why didn't you kill me?"

Again I said, "Can we help you?" And she said no. She didn't want to be helped. Life had been unfair to her. Someone had treated her terribly. She was mad at the world and mad at God.

I asked, "Can we take you back in town?" She replied, "No, leave me alone. I don't want to be helped." She started cursing the police and everyone else. And then she just took off running down the road. I couldn't just leave her there going down the road. People were going by and cars were speeding down the road. No one was stopping to help.

Daniel and I went into town and got the police. But when we returned she had disappeared. No one could find her. She had run into the night hoping to die because life was unfair.

People commit suicide because life is unfair. At times, they hurt themselves or others because no justice can be found.

That young woman was just one of a multitude of people who cry out that life isn't fair. She is just one who is hurting, crying, and wanting to die because she thinks life is unfair. Maybe people such as her do not like the family they were born into, or the neighborhood in which they live. Maybe they do not like the color of their skin. Maybe they hate the economic status of their parents and their upbringing. So they look around, mad at God and everyone else, crying out, "Why? Why? Why?"

Have you ever felt that life was unfair? Have you ever been treated unfairly by a spouse, parent, child, or business associate? At times, you may feel overlooked, offended, and completely misused by others. I know that life at times is unfair, but God is always fair and just.

God cares about you. It does not matter where you've been. Nor does it matter what you have done. The Blood of Jesus Christ is more powerful then anything you have done and anywhere you have been.

God Is Just and Righteous

The people of God were facing the darkest hour in the history of their nation. The kingdom of Judah was about to be carried into captivity by Babylon. The prophet Jeremiah was weeping over his beloved country and its capital city, Jerusalem. Tragic suffering beset both a people and a prophet. So sorrowful and distressed was Jeremiah that he cried out, "Is there no balm in Gilead, is there no physician there? Why then is not the health of the daughter of my people recovered?"

As well as Jeremiah knew God, he nonetheless cried out with questions of "Why?" He could not understand why God's people did not repent of their sin and return to Jehovah. He could not understand how God could allow His covenant people to be carried off into captivity. It seemed that God was not keeping His covenant. Jeremiah couldn't understand God. No answers seemed to fit the situation when God said, "Let not the wise man glory in his wisdom, neither let the mighty man glory in his might, let not the rich man glory in his riches: but let him that glorieth glory in this, that he understandeth and knoweth me, that I am the Lord which exercise lovingkindness, judgment, and righteousness, in the earth: for in these things I delight, saith the Lord" (Jer. 9:23–24).

Notice that even when Jeremiah could not figure out why God was doing certain things, he had one certainty that He could hold onto—God. When facing suffering, wisdom does not help nor do might or riches. Only knowing God can see us through the darkest nights of the soul. No matter how dark the night, deep the trouble, or trying the trial, God is there. And He is just, righteous, and loving.

Out of the traumatic tragedy of Judah's defeat and exile, God revealed Himself to Jeremiah as Jehovah–Tsedeknu, "the Lord Our Righteousness" (Jer. 23:6). Righteousness and justice go hand in hand. When we talk about God being righteous, we are talking about God also being just. We don't serve a mean God or an unfair God. Now we do live in an unfair world. Has life been unfair to you? Has a mate been unfair to you? Have you been abused by someone, maybe a parent or a husband? Have you been overlooked and left out and hurt and offended? Many unfair things happen in the work force. Many cutbacks and restructuring of companies are causing people to lose their life savings or having to work harder for less money.

Because people experience injustice in life, they may begin to believe that God is unfair. Human nature has a tendency to blame God for every problem. Jeremiah refused to blame God for his problems or the turmoil in his nation. He knew that sin had shipwrecked his life and his nation.

Do you know why you and I have problems today in our lives? The first reason is sin. I'm talking about the original sin. If things are happening in your life that are unfair, look first to your sin or the sin of those around you as the cause. When man sinned he released a curse on this earth. That curse is sickness, heartache, pain, disease, and turmoil. All those things are a result of the sin.

It's impossible for God to be unfair to us.

Secondly, life is unfair because of ignorance. When we act without knowing God, we experience the consequences of that ignorance. God wants us to make wise decisions based on knowing Him. Often painful situations we call unfair are simply the consequences of making ignorant decisions. When we act unwisely, we need to accept responsibility for our own decisions and not blame God for injustice in life.

God is just and good. In Revelation 16:5, God is revealed as being righteous. Notice, God always has been just. He is never unfair.

God cannot be bribed. God cannot be bought off. He judges the whole earth. Human judges, from time to time, can be bribed. But God's judgments are always righteous, fair, and just.

"After that I heard what sounded like a shout of a vast throng, like the boom of many pounding waves and like the roar of terrific and mighty thunderpeal, exclaiming, Hallelujah—praise the Lord! For now the Lord our God, the Omnipotent, the All–Ruler reigns." (Rev. 19:6, AMP). God is the judge and the ruler over all the earth. He is all–powerful. He is all–just. He can never be wrong. He can never do wrong. Nothing is ever His fault. He is a just God.

Again in Revelation 15:3, we see that the omnipotent God is both righteous and just. Is He your King today? Then, He'll never do you wrong today. Mark it down. Take it to the bank. He cannot act unjustly. It's impossible for God to do you wrong. It's impossible for God to be unfair. It's impossible for Him to be bribed or bought off or manipulated to do wrong in your life. He is a just and good God.

When we know God to be just and righteous, we are to recognize Him as that and to sing praises about His righteousness just as the choirs of glory sing in the book of Revelation. The world may be unfair, but we can know His righteousness no matter what the circumstance.

When we know God, one thing we learn is that God is fair when life isn't. Yes, life is unfair. Yes, people are unfair. They are cruel. But God is not a mean God. God is a good God. God is a just God.

Give your life to Him and let Him heal you, forgive you, and give you a new beginning. Find out that He's a good God and I tell you, you'll want to live. Find out He's a just God and cannot be anything but fair. Because He is always righteous and just, He is worthy to be worshiped, served, loved, and known.

When life is unfair, choose to look to the just and fair God. When life is filled with lemons, make lemonade. Wherever you are planted, bloom there. Instead of letting the devil beat, bruise, and batter you, turn to the Lord God your righteousness.

God Is Our Rock

Deuteronomy 32:4 calls God *our rock*. What does that mean? He is stable. He is sound. You can give your life to Him. You can build your life around Him and upon Him. As the rock, God's judgment and justice are perfect. People may not be perfect and life certainly isn't. But God is perfect.

Faith is not built on life's fairness but God's goodness and righteousness. Conventional wisdom says, "Life is hard, and then we die." Godly wisdom knows that though life is hard, God is just and good. We may not have all the answers to life's injustices but we serve the One who does. Too many people fill their lives with questions asking "why?" causing bitterness in response to life's mysterious difficulties. You could spend your entire life asking:

- Why am I this way?
- Why do I look this way?
- Why do I have this kind of personality?
- Why was I raised this way?
- Why do I live here?
- Why was I raised in this Country, this Nation, or this particular area?

- Why did my baby or my loved one die? Why are there wars?
- Why do people divorce and destroy their families?
- Why is does disease exist?

If you answer that God caused any of these tragic things, then you do not know Him. To know God is to know that He is both just and good. He does not author evil or cause suffering. We live in a sin–infested world of our own making and the making of generations before us.

So when you feel isolated, lonely and unloved, and you want to lay down in the middle of the road and end it all, don't go from one hell to another. Don't do that! Know that there is a God who created you with a divine destiny. God believes in you.

Reasons Why There Is Suffering

Let me summarize for you some of the reasons why bad things happen to good people and why life may seem unfair. This is not an exhaustive list, but it may help you through your questions:

1. **The root cause of suffering is sin.** When we suffer, it may be the consequence of our own sin or the sin of someone else.

2. **Suffering is often caused by ignorance.** We make mistakes out of ignorance. Those mistakes and failures often hurt us and those around us.

3. **Suffering pours out of a sinful world.** The world we live in has been polluted by sin. Disease and pain have permeated the fabric of creation. All creation groans for the salvation and healing of Christ (Rom. 8). Just living in this sinful world makes us the target of evil.

4. **Suffering results from persecution.** Jesus warns us that in this world we will have tribulation (John 16:33). But He also assures us that we will overcome those trials through Him. Rejoice when you are persecuted for His name's sake. Though hated by the world, your blessing comes from a just and good God who holds this world in judgment.

5. **Suffering comes from the fiery darts of the devil.** The devil seeks to steal, kill, and destroy. Though under attack, the Word of your testimony and the blood of the Lamb will ultimately defeat Satan (Rev. 12:11).

Major on Your Blessings not Your Battles

In the Bible, the man aside from Christ who experienced the greatest suffering was Job. He grew greatly in his knowledge of God as he suffered. The incredible benefit and lesson that he gained from knowing God through suffering was: *major on your blessings not your battles.* Let's explore this together.

The battle you are in today is not over your past nor it is over your present.

Remember how Pharaoh tried to kill all the young children? Moses was attacked when he was just a few months old. That battle wasn't over his past but over his future. Why? Because at age eighty, Moses became the mighty leader and champion for God leading the people of Israel out of Egypt.

The battle that you are in today is over your future.

The same was true about Jesus. When Herod killed all the babies under two years old in Bethlehem that battle was not over Jesus' past but His future. Why? Because at age thirty–three He would be the crucified Lord and risen Savior of the world.

The battle that you are in today doesn't concern your past. The past is past. The battle that you are in is not over the present. The present is present. But the battle that you are fighting today is over your future: what God has scheduled for you. What God wants to do in you. What God wants to do through you, and what God wants to do for you.

Take note of this: If the battle is over your future, then we could say Satan evidently believes that your future is worth fighting *for.*

The battles, sufferings, and struggles you face today are proof that your future is bright because the battle is not over your past; it's not over your present; the battle is over your future. If Satan believes your future is worth a fight, then surely you and I should believe our future is worth fighting *for*.

If you are in a battle, suffering, and feeling weary, consider the end of Job. Don't consider the battle, but consider the end of Job. Look at Job 42:5, "Then Job answered the Lord and said, I have heard of thee by the hearing of the ear." Please underline that phrase, *heard of thee*.

Job had heard of God but still didn't know Him personally. What do I mean? Well, I can't live on someone else's book, someone else's tape, someone else's revelation. What they have heard of God can educate and inform me but never empower me. Only knowing God personally can empower me to face all that life throws at me.

Major on your blessings and minor on your battles.

My grandmother was a great woman of God. She knew God. I have been told that my grandmother would hold me as a baby in her arms on that little farm in southern Iowa. She would hold me in her arms and pray over my life. She would prophesy over my life. She would pray, "God use him for the ministry. Use him for your work." She was a wonderful woman of God. She died on a Sunday night in church while singing praises to God. The people say she was seated in the pew, with both hands lifted, worshiping God. They saw her just gently lean over in the pew and pass away to go to glory. What a wonderful heritage.

What a wonderful grandmother. But as great as she was I can't live on her faith. I can't live on what she heard of God. I can't live on what she knew of God.

Now Job didn't stop with just hearing of God. He proceeded to say, "But now mine eye seeth Thee" (Job 42:5b). Once you have seen the Lord and known Him personally, your perspective on suffering, trials, and battles changes forever.

Something happens when you move from hearing about Jesus to seeing Jesus for yourself. O that I might see Him and that smile upon His face. There is nothing like having an encounter with Jesus. He really is *all you need*. He really is.

I have asked people when they are suffering, "What do you believe you need?" Some have said, "A financial miracle." Others replied, "I need a healing." Some answered, "I need my wife or my husband or my children back." Job had lost his children, lost his possessions, lost his health, and lost the respect of his wife and friends. Yet, he did not ask to have any of that back. All he longed for was to see God. He didn't need to know why all the tragedy had befallen him. All he needed to know was God.

Once you see and know the Lord and once you taste and see that the Lord is good, the suffering and battles fade and the blessings come. Consider Job's end. After the tragic losses, after the ridicule of wife and friends, after crying out to God, he dialogued with God and spiritually saw God. Hearing from and knowing God personally changed Job's life. After Job saw God, he saw himself as he really was, "Wherefore I abhor myself, and repent in dust and ashes" (Job 42:6).

After knowing God and repenting, Job saw his battle transformed into a blessing. Job was not only blessed but he also began to pray for his friends to be blessed (Job 42:10).

Are you in the midst of a battle filled with suffering, pain, and difficult? Get your eyes off the battle and on the Lord. See Him. Allow yourself and your pride to be broken. Accept whatever God has for you. And then watch the Lord win your battle, shower you with blessings, and give you a heart to bless others.

When you suffer, don't withdraw from God. Like Job, refuse to curse or blame God. Instead of asking *why*, run to Him. As you draw close to God, you will see Him as a just and good God. As you come to know Him, you will discover these wonderful benefits and blessings:

- God is just and good.
- Life is unfair but that's not God's fault.
- Bad things do happen to good people because we live in an evil and unjust world.
- God's justice and righteousness will triumph over injustice.

If you are struggling with a circumstance that you regard as unjust or unfair, turn to the God who is just and pray:

Almighty God,
You alone are just and good.
Though I do not understand all the
"whys" of life,
I ask you to see me through life
knowing that Your justice and righteous
will ultimately overcome all evil.
Amen.

CHAPTER 9

GOD: THE OMNIPRESENT ONE

"Am I a God at hand, saith the Lord, and not a God afar
off? Can any hide himself in secret places that
I shall not see him? saith the Lord. Do not
I fill heaven and earth? saith the Lord."
JEREMIAH 23:23–24

Growing up I couldn't get away with anything. My mom seemed to have a remarkable intuition of knowing where I was at any time of the day or night. Invariably when I would change my destination from what I told her to a different place—without calling to tell her—she would call the first place just to check on me. If I had gone somewhere without telling her or calling to tell her a change of plans, then hold on. I was in big trouble. Beyond that, just when I didn't want my friends to know that Mom knew what I was doing, she would show up at the mall or the school event, and I would die of embarrassment. It seemed that Mom could be anywhere and everywhere anytime she wanted.

Of course, we know that moms are not omnipresent, yet the Father is. God the Father is everywhere all the time. Whenever we need Him, He's there. Even when we don't want Him to see us and what we are doing, there God is. God is omnipresent—everywhere all the time.

Jeremiah 23 reveals that no secret place is hidden from God. He is everywhere and sees everything at all times. That's omnipresence. God never has to be somewhere because God is everywhere. There never was a time God wasn't everywhere. God is not bound by space and time. God is everywhere. He's omnipresent. "Am I a God at hand, saith the Lord, and not a God afar off? Can any hide himself in secret places that I shall not see him? saith the Lord. Do not I fill the heaven and I fill the earth with His Presence, saith the Lord" (Jer. 23:23). God is everywhere. God is there before I am there. God is Omnipresent. He is everywhere.

Have you ever been somewhere with a family member and experienced a very meaningful time with them? And then you came back to that place years later without that person but you still felt their presence when you were in that place? What you felt was really the relationship you had with them. Relationship brings us into the presence of another person. So we enter into the presence of God through a relationship that is built on knowing Him.

Going back to Psalm 139:1, we see that relationship and omnipresence go hand in hand. David says, "O Lord thou hast searched me, and known me." We are known by God for He is everywhere, even inside of us, searching our hearts by His Spirit.

God understands what you are thinking at this moment. Through His omnipresence He is also all-knowing. According to Psalm 139, God knows what we are going to speak, for He knows our thoughts. He knows when we rise and when we lie down. God knows what we are going to do before we do it. He knows all of our ways.

Now, we can look at that negatively and say, "Oh no, God knows all the bad that is in my life." But look at the positive side for a moment. God knows your walk. In other words, God knows every act of service and work you do for Him. God knows the words we are going to speak. What we say is important to God. So, if God knows our talk, then God knows when we are praising Him because that is talk. God knows not only when we curse, but also when we praise Him. That's exciting. If when no one else knows the good we do, it doesn't really matter. God knows and that is what matters.

God knows our walk and our talk.

Psalm 139 reveals that no place in the universe, not even hell, is void of the presence of God. I love the name of God that speaks of His omnipresence: Jehovah–Shammah—the Lord is There (Ez. 48:35). Wherever you are or go, He compasses you about and surrounds you with His Spirit.

Five Incredible Benefits From His Omnipotence

We tap into God's omnipresence through a relationship with Him...knowing God. What are the benefits of being in His presence?

#1 — In His presence, you will flee sin. Consider Joseph (Gen. 39). He is tempted by Potiphar's wife to commit adultery with her. But God's favor and presence were with Joseph. God was there in Potiphar's house with Joseph just as

He was with Him in the pit and in Jacob's house. God's presence gave Joseph the strength and conviction to flee from sin. Considering sin? Flee all immorality, for God sees every thought and action.

He is there with you in the motel room, the backseat of a car, and in the video store. He sees the remote control for the TV in your hands and knows what channel you are watching. God sees every look you cast toward the opposite sex and knows every fantasy on the silver screen of your mind. So, flee immorality for you are in His presence. Before you stick a needle in your arm, take a drink, smoke dope or shoplift a desired object, remember that God is there. Integrity is what you do when no one else is looking but God. Sure you may have integrity in the presence of humans you are trying to impress with your spirituality, but do you have integrity in the presence of God where no human can see?

Before you sin remember that whatever you do, you are performing on the stage of eternity before an audience of one— Almighty God.

Before you sin, ask yourself, "Can I do this with God looking?" Knowing that Jehovah–Shammah, God is There, will empower you to say "No!" to sin.

#2 — God's omnipresence makes me accountable. If He sees all my steps, then He knows when I go to

church and when I don't. He knows when I gave my word
and kept my promise and when I broke my promise. He sees
all my steps. He knows all my ways. God holds me accountable by His presence as a spouse, a parent, an employer or
employee, a church volunteer and a witness for Christ.

Let me get personal here. Jesus says that the way we
treat the "least of these" (Matt. 25), we treat Him. If God
knows all my ways, then I better start treating all the people
around me right. That includes how I treat my family, my col-
leagues at work, people around me at church and those in the
neighborhood. I must put in a full day's work for my salary
and be honest on my expense account and taxes. I must
speak with respect to waiters and waitresses. I must treat the
mechanic, plumber, hairdresser, and store clerk as I would
treat the Lord. God is watching. His omnipresence holds me
accountable. Accountable is not a dirty word because it is part
of obedience. Accountability opens the door to God's anoint-
ing and power in my life. Are you accountable to the God
who is there?

#3 — God's omnipresence causes fear to flee.
"Let your conversation be without covetousness: and be con-
tent with such things as ye have: for he hath said I will never
leave thee, and I will never forsake thee. And I will not fear
what man shall do unto me." (Heb. 13:5–6). Because God is
there I have no fear of any person or demon. Since God is
omnipresent, He is there before I get there. He is in tomorrow before I get there. So, there's nothing to fear in
tomorrow. That's good news. Before a problem or question in
my life arrives, He is there with the answer. There is no problem or question about life that I fear. God is there.

#4 — Knowing the Omnipresent God empowers me to endure all of life's trials and tribulations. First Peter 2:19 says, "For this is thankworthy, if a man for conscience toward God [aware of God's presence] endure grief, suffering wrongly."

Because God is there, I won't give up, throwing up my hands and walking away. When things are hard, I will endure and keep on keeping on. I will not quit when the devil throws up my past. I will not quit when the devil says I am a failure. I will not quit when the devil tells me it's too late. I will not quit when the accuser tries to magnify my mistakes. I will not quit when times get tough. In the Lord, I'm tough, and when times get tough, the tough keep going.

Knowing that God is with me will cause me to persevere through any trial.

When your conscience is aware of God, then you know that He is seeing you through everything. Through a relationship you realize that because God is with you, you will endure. Knowing God gets you through whatever you are going through. Knowing that He is faithful, knowing that He is all–knowing, He is all–powerful, He is good, He is kind, He is holy, He is there and will strengthen you to endure whatever you are going through so that you will not quit. You will endure criticism and accusations, refusing to take the bait of Satan and pick up an offense. Because God is there, you will endure.

#5 — Because God is there, you will be able to make right decisions. Proverbs 3:5–6 says, "Do not lean unto your own understanding but acknowledge God in all your ways and He will direct your paths and crown them with success." What are you doing? You are acknowledging God in every one of life's decisions so that you can make the right decisions and walk the right paths.

God is there in your decision–making. He is present to help you choose right over wrong. Acknowledging His presence gives you the wisdom and boldness to do what is right.

The incredible benefits of knowing God as omnipresent are:

- the power to flee sin.
- a relationship of ultimate accountability to God.
- fear being caused to flee in His presence.
- endurance to go through anything in life.
- the ability to make right decision when acknowledging His presence.

If you need to know that God is omnipresent in your life right now, then pray:

O omnipresent God,
I praise You for being there at all times,
in all places to meet all my needs.
Make me sensitive to Your presence so that
I may flee sin, be accountable to You,
endure every trial, overcome every fear,
and acknowledge Your right way in my every decision.
Thank You, Lord, for always being there.
Amen.

CONCLUSION

KNOWING GOD THE FATHER

"If ye had known me, ye should have known my Father also:
and from henceforth ye know him, and have seen him"
(JOHN 14:7)

Throughout this book we have developed these three priorities for life:

#1 — Knowing God is the foundation for our lives.
#2 — Knowing God shapes our lives.
#3 — Knowing God is the goal of our lives.

In Jeremiah 9:23–24 we discovered the pursuit of both the natural and the spiritual person. Setting aside natural pursuits, the Christian's life pursuit is to know God so that we can make Him known to others.

What happens to people when they really begin to know God? Paul gives us an insight into the results that are produced from knowing God. "Him we preach and proclaim, warning and admonishing every one and instructing every one in all wisdom, [in comprehensive insight into the ways and purposes of God], that we may present every person mature—full grown, fully initiated, complete and perfect—in Christ, the anointed one" (Col. 1:29, AMP). What is that saying?

Maturity is a result of a relationship, not age. Churches teach people the Word not so that

The more that we know God, the more we will mature in Him.

Christians will simply know *about* Him. They teach the Word so that we will understand His ways, His plans, and His purposes in our lives. So in understanding God—His nature and operation—we will become full grown, mature and perfect in Christ.

Remember the process of growth that comes in knowing God.

- To know God is to love Him.
- To love God is to obey Him.
- To obey God is to fellowship and abide with Him.
- To abide with God produces fruitfulness in our lives.

Now people who have a hard time worshiping or praying for an hour or two, obviously do not know God and are not growing toward completeness and wholeness in Christ. Yes, they may be saved, but knowing God is a growing relationship that lasts a lifetime. Just a thought: If people have a hard time with an hour and a half in the presence of God, what are they going to do throughout eternity in the presence of God?

How do we know God? How do we have a relationship with Him? We have seen from the Word of God that we have a relationship with the Father through faith in His Son, Jesus Christ. We know the Father through His Word, His names, His attributes, obedience, worship and praise, and through creation.

To know God is to have a relationship with Him as your heavenly Father. "Yet for us there is [only] one God, the Father, Who is the Source of all things, and for Whom we [have life], and one Lord, Jesus Christ, through and by Whom we [ourselves exist]" (1 Cor. 9:6, AMP).

God our Father has exclusive claim and status in our lives. There is no one like Him. My job is not my God. My family is not my God. There is only one God, the Father, who is the source of all things for whom we have life. The source of all happiness and joy in life is God the Father.

Happiness is not a result of a geographical location. True happiness is the result of a relationship with the Father through the Lord Jesus Christ. In Him everything exists including happiness.

We have come to understand that God the Father is:

- Self–existing and eternal.
- All–knowing.
- Never–changing.
- All–powerful.
- Faithful.
- Just and good.
- Omnipresent.

So what kind of Father is He? As we bring our study to a close, let's return to the Scriptures to discover the incredible benefits of knowing God as our Father.

The Incredible Benefits of Knowing the Father

God wants us to be His children and a part of His family. Our Father desires that we belong to Him and be in the Family of God. So here are the incredible benefits that come from knowing Him as Father.

1. As our Father, God rewards us. (Heb. 11:6) He loves to give good gifts to His children.

2. As our Father, God disciplines us. (Heb. 12:7) Discipline is not punishment but rather teaching and correcting. (Heb. 12:7)

3. As our Father, God listens to us. (Matt. 6:6, 18:19) God not only listens, but He also answers every prayer and meets every need.

4. As our Father, God knows us intimately. (Matt. 6:8) God knows us from the inside out. He knows every thought, feeling and action.

5. As our Father, God is aware of our needs and understands how to meet them. (Mt. 6:8; Phil. 4:19) God *meets* our needs, but delights in *giving* us our wants according to His will. He knows our hurts and heals them.

6. As our Father, God loves us. (1 John 3:1) He loves us just the way we are and loves us too much to leave us the way we are.

7. As our Father, God gives us good gifts. (Luke 11:13) God does not give evil gifts nor does He do bad things to us. He is the giver of every good gift (James 1:17).

8. As our Father, God judges our work. (1 Pet. 1:17) God examines our hearts, convicts us of sin and commands us to live holy lives. He alone judges and reproves us by His Word.

9. As our Father, God sets an example for us. (Matt. 5:43) In Christ, God has shown us how to live. He is the potter and we are the clay (Isa. 64:8). God never gives up on us and patiently works with us through every situation in life.

10. As our Father, God is no respecter of persons. (1 Pet. 1:17) He shows no favoritism. He does not love one person more than others. He generously showers His grace upon all of us.

God the Father desires an intimate relationship with you. Through His Son, Jesus Christ, God has provided the way for you to come to Him. Jesus' shed blood on the cross makes it possible for you to come the Father. Through the Holy Spirit, God has revealed Himself in Scripture and is seeking us out to know Him.

God the Father has planned for eternity that you have a relationship with Him. God the Son has created the universe and brought you into being by the power of His Word. He has saved you and sent His Spirit to empower, guide, and direct your life. God the Spirit reveals His plan and purpose to you while helping you accomplish His will.

I am praying that you have met and come to know God as you have journeyed with me through these pages. You have discovered the incredible benefits that come from knowing God.

Knowing God is the first priority of life. Knowing God is the foundation of life. Knowing God is the goal of life. Pursue Him as the deer pants and thirsts for water. Desire Him as a lover longs for a mate. Hunger for Him as a starving beggar seeks bread. But more than everything else, know Him as the lover of your soul. May this be your prayer:

As the deer pants for the water brooks,
So pants my soul for You, O God.
My soul thirsts for God, for the living God.
Why are you cast down, O my soul?
And why are you disquieted within me?
Hope in God; For I shall yet praise Him,
The help of my countenance and my God.
Father, I am still, that I might know You.
Be still my soul and know God.
Father, I desire to know You with my whole heart.
Amen.

[ADAPTED FROM PSALMS 42 AND 46]

5 Benefits of the New Covenant

1. forgiveness of sin

2. fullness of the Holy Spirit

3. Soundness – health + healing

4. Success – freedom from curse of law
   – poverty, fear, death

5. Security – freedom from fear of
   death + hell.

Additional copies of
The Incredible Benefits of Knowing God
are available at fine bookstores everywhere
or directly from:

Church On The Rock
P. O. Box 1668
St. Peters. MO 63376-8668

About The Author

Pastor David Blunt and his wife, Kim, are the pastors of Church On The Rock in St. Peters, Missouri. From the days of its small beginning of only 35 people back in 1983, God has had His hand on this ministry. Today, Church On The Rock is a dynamic, growing church of over 3,000 members that strives to impact its city and the world with the Gospel of Jesus Christ.

Pastor Blunt's insights into the Word challenge and inspire believers to grow to new levels in their relationship with God and their service to others. His practical, personable style of teaching causes the Word to come alive in the hearts of people and draws them into a personal encounter with Jesus. This life–changing ministry is committed to raising up and equipping believers to answer the call of God on their lives and to become all that He created them to be.

Also available from David Blunt are the following inspiring tape series:

Authority of the Believer
Wisdom for Winning in Life
God's Love the Way to Win

Send all prayer requests and inquiries to:

Pastor David Blunt
Church On The Rock
P. O. Box 1668
St. Peters, MO 63376-8668